MAGIC & MALADIES

STARRY HOLLOW WITCHES, BOOK 10

ANNABEL CHASE

RED PALM PRESS LLC

CHAPTER ONE

What's so fascinating out there? Raoul asked. His claws clicked on the windowsill as he moved closer for a better view.

"Alec agreed to walk the dog and it's a standoff," I said. "They're just staring at each other like it's High Noon and one of them has to shoot first." It was anyone's guess as to which one had better aim. The aging Yorkshire terrier might have trouble climbing onto the bed, but he could pinpoint the prettiest flower on the bush with deadly accuracy.

Why is the vampire walking him?

"I'd like them to bond," I said. "I think the dog feels threatened by Alec and I'm hoping to change that with some quality time."

Pretty sure a lot of us feel threatened by him. The dude's a scary bloodsucker. Raoul brightened. *Hey, maybe he should take me out for pizza so we can bond, too.*

I looked down at him in amazement. "You really don't have scruples, do you?"

Not when it comes to free pizza. Raoul paused. *His nickname shouldn't be PP3. Heck, it isn't even PP1. The dog's dehydrated.*

"He's not dehydrated. He's just stubborn." I could see that

1

Alec's patience was running out, so I left the cottage to relieve him of urinary duty.

Alec gave me a helpless look, which was strikingly sexy on the usually confident vampire. "I'm afraid I may not be cut out for pet ownership." He handed over the leash.

"Prescott Peabody the third," I admonished him. "You've already sniffed that blade of grass fifty times. Let's pick up the pace."

The terrier didn't spare me a glance. He continued his search for the ideal spot to urinate.

"Even the one ring to rule them all only had to be thrown into the fires of Mount Doom," I continued impatiently. "There wasn't a particular spot. Just anywhere was A-Okay."

PP3 wandered over to an entirely new section of grass and started the search again.

"Just keep him away from my garden," Marley called from a nearby picnic blanket. She and Bonkers were strengthening their familiar bond by playing games that her teacher at the Black Cloak Academy had recommended.

I rolled my eyes. "Yes, yes. The sacred herb garden shall be protected from PP3's bodily fluids."

"While we're on the topic of bodily fluids," Alec began in a low voice.

I silenced him with a look. "You know the answer to that."

PP3 finally chose a spot and I praised him loudly and gave his head a scratch. He didn't have the best hearing anymore, so I wanted to make sure he got the message of approval.

"I should go," Alec said. "The dentist awaits."

I smiled. "I love that you have to go to the dentist."

He seemed mildly affronted. "I have dental needs, the same as anyone with teeth or fangs."

"Have you ever had a cavity in one of your fangs?" I asked. "Maybe too much sugar in the blood?"

He didn't bother to reply. He simply bent forward and brushed his lips against mine. "I look forward to tomorrow."

I was so distracted by the kiss that I blanked out everything else until PP3 began tugging me toward the house.

"Bye, Alec." Marley ran over and threw her arms around his waist.

He gave her hair an affectionate ruffle and waved to Raoul. "Farewell, bandit friend."

Hey, he acknowledged me. That's progress.

I admired Alec's long strides as he returned to his car and drove away. Sometimes I still wanted to pinch myself.

"Um, Mom. What's that?"

I turned to look at her, still lost in inappropriate thoughts. "Huh? What?"

Marley pointed to the right side of Rose Cottage where a tall post covered in tufty, lime-green carpet stood.

"What the Elvis?" I looped the end of PP3's leash onto a fence post. As I moved closer to investigate, Raoul intercepted me.

Oh, right. I forgot to mention I came bearing gifts, Raoul said. *I could use a little help moving this into the house.*

I laughed. "I'm sorry. What now?"

The raccoon tapped the green monstrosity. *I won this at the dump. You have no idea how hard I had to work for this one.*

"You won this?" I repeated. "You mean you weren't the only one in the entire universe that wanted it?"

It was me against Russo, that tuxedo cat I told you about. He shook his head. *If he hadn't been declawed, he totally could have schooled me.*

"Why did you think bringing it here was a good plan?"

Raoul gestured to the picnic blanket. *I thought Bonkers might like it. Marley always has her so busy with all that learning, I thought this would be nice for her to just chill on.*

"Raoul, that's so…"

Unlike me? I know. I hardly recognize myself anymore in that cracked mirror at the entrance to the dump.

"I was going to say sweet, but whatever." I called to Marley. "Raoul has something to show you and Bonkers."

Marley scurried over with the flying kitten hovering above her shoulder. Bonkers didn't wait for an explanation. She landed on one of the platforms and immediately began digging her claws into the green carpet.

"Thank you so much, Raoul," Marley said. "This was really thoughtful." She looked at me, her blue eyes hopeful. "Can I bring this in the house? It'll get ruined if it stays outside."

"I think it passed ruined about two shades of green ago, but go ahead."

Marley dragged the post around the corner toward the front door with Bonkers flying beside her.

I spun around to confront my raccoon familiar. "Okay, buddy. Spill it. What's your actual motivation?"

Raoul flashed me an innocent look. *Kindness. Selflessness. What other motivation is there?*

I folded my arms and fixed him with a hard stare. "Greed. Selfishness. Diversion."

Raoul's body sagged. *I've never been so insulted.*

"Now I know for a fact that isn't true."

Raoul scampered toward the house. *I swear on my favorite uncle's grave that my motives are pure. I thought Bonkers would enjoy it.*

I suddenly felt embarrassed for assuming the worst about Raoul. I knew he was capable of selfless behavior because I'd been the recipient of it on more than one occasion.

"I'm sorry I doubted you," I said.

I crossed the front yard to reclaim PP3 from the fence. The dog was rolling on his back across a row of Marley's carefully planted herbs.

"PP3, no," I said firmly. He usually only rolled on snakeskin or worms. My fingers were crossed for worms. I unhooked him from the post and started to walk him into the house.

Raoul glanced skyward. *I think that bird is trying to get your attention.*

"Nice try, Raoul." A white dove swooped down and dropped an envelope at my feet. I screamed and jumped back, landing smack on a section of the herb garden.

Told you so.

The dove flew away and I stepped out of the garden. Hopefully Marley was too busy with the new scratching post to witness my infraction. She was taking this garden very seriously, which was good for her, but nerve-racking for me. I was destined to destroy it the way I destroyed all living things.

Raoul swiped the envelope and tore it open.

I held my hand out, palm open. "Excuse me. Is that addressed to you?"

How should I know? I'm a raccoon. I can't read.

I snatched the envelope from his hand. "It's a reminder about Bentley and Meadow's wedding." Only Bentley would be so uptight as to send a reminder for his wedding. If the elf could have gotten RSVPs in blood, he probably would have.

Ooh, I love weddings. When is it?

"Tomorrow and you're not invited. Humans only."

What kind of lame party is that? he huffed.

"No kids either, actually," I said.

Good. Then Marley, Bonkers, and I will order a pizza and watch Wall-E, Raoul said.

One screening of Wall-E and the raccoon was hooked. He even had a recurring dream where his alien overlords arrived and delivered him to a planet covered in garbage.

"I don't know about leaving the three of you in charge of the house that long," I said.

Hey, I don't know about leaving you in charge, yet it still seems to happen all the time.

"You make a solid argument." I tucked the reminder into my pocket and steered PP3 back to the cottage.

That night, I walked alone through a hazel and willow tunnel. Tendrils of ivy curled around the base of the tunnel, threatening to make their way to the top.

"Marley?" I called.

No one answered. I peered ahead and saw only darkness. I turned to look over my shoulder from the place I came. More shadows. It seemed as though I existed between two black holes.

"Raoul?"

My familiar didn't respond.

"Alec, are you here?"

The vampire was nowhere to be seen.

I felt so completely alone. It was a terrifying feeling, as though everyone in my life had abandoned me.

I ran through the tunnel as my heart thundered in my chest, but the more distance I covered, the farther away the end appeared. The tunnel seemed to elongate with every step. There was no point in going backward. It seemed much too far away now. I shot a fist to the side and tried to punch my way through the tunnel. The hazel and willow held firm. When I withdrew my fist, I saw that my knuckles were bloody.

"Somebody help me!" My words echoed in the void. In that moment, I wanted to raze the picturesque tunnel—burn it to the ground. The feeling was primal, probably because I felt like a caged animal.

I began to kick and tear at the sides of the tunnel, screaming and grunting with every move. It was horrible to feel so…contained. So restrained. It was unnatural.

Another swift kick and a bone in my foot cracked. I cried out in pain and staggered to my knees.

"Help," I said, but the word was strangled by my sobs. I buried my face in my hands and wept.

As the first tear hit the ground, the earth opened its mouth and swallowed me whole. My body plunged into a cave filled with gleaming treasures. Gemstones twinkled and gold glittered. When I glanced upward, there was no evidence of the hole I'd fallen through. I looked around helplessly. There were mounds of valuables, but no sign of life.

I climbed over a hill of jewels to see the remains of a body on the other side. The skeleton was perfectly preserved, its back against the cave wall in a seated position. Bony arms were wrapped around bonier knees. It seemed eerily calm, as though the living creature had simply sat down and waited for death until it mercifully arrived.

At the sight of the composed skeleton, I did the only thing I could think of.

I let out a bloodcurdling scream.

"Mom?"

I blinked the sleep from my eyes to see Marley's silhouette framed in the doorway. "Marley?"

"Are you okay?"

"What time is it?"

"I don't know," she said. "The middle of the night."

I pulled myself to a seated position. "What are you doing here?" I mumbled. "Did you have a nightmare?"

"No, but it sounds like you did." She came to sit on the edge of my bed. "You yelled so loud that you woke me up."

"I did?"

"You even scared PP3." She reached toward the foot of the bed and gave him a reassuring scratch behind the ears.

"He looks unruffled to me." In fact, the aging dog looked like he was still asleep. "What did I yell?"

"Help is what I heard," Marley said. "Someone help me." She bit her lip. "Do you think it's the wedding?"

"Why would a wedding give me nightmares?" I asked.

"Maybe you're anxious about going to a wedding with Alec." I covered her hand with mine and she pulled away to wipe her hand on the covers. "Your palms are sweaty."

"Sweaty palms aside, weddings don't give me anxiety," I said. "Weddings are fun. Open bar and music on the beach? That's my kind of party."

"Yes, but will Granger be there?" she asked quietly.

"No, he's not invited," I replied. "You don't have to worry about him, honey. He's a grown man and he can take care of himself."

"I'm not worried about him," Marley said. "I just wondered if you are."

I tried to remember my dream—or nightmare, but I couldn't conjure any details. "He's a handsome werewolf with a heart of gold. I bet he'll be dating someone new in no time."

"Maybe it was an anxiety dream about the spell you're supposed to perform at the wedding."

Crap-on-a-stick. I'd forgotten about the spell. I mean, I'd practiced it, but probably not as often as I should have.

"That's probably it." I patted her hand. "You go back to sleep, okay?"

"Should I sleep in here with you in case you have another nightmare?" Marley didn't wait for a response. She scrambled across my legs and peeled back the covers on the other side of the bed.

"I guess I wouldn't mind the company," I said weakly.

There was no point in arguing. I had years of experience co-sleeping with Marley and, for the most part, she now slept all night in her own bed.

Marley fluffed the pillow and made herself comfortable as she curled up beside me. "Just like old times, right, Mom?"

"I feel safer already with a powerful witch beside me," I said, and closed my eyes to go back to sleep.

CHAPTER TWO

ALEC'S DRIVER dropped us off at the entrance to Balefire Beach and we made our way toward the makeshift wedding venue. Dozens of white chairs with white ribbons were set up on the beach facing the water. A white gazebo was positioned between the chairs and the shoreline. I sure hoped someone had taken high tide into account when planning this ceremony or we'd be watching the exchange of vows surrounded by a pod of dolphins.

We reached the area of the beach where a small crowd was gathered, waiting to be seated.

"Don't you look dapper?" I said, admiring Alec's perfect physique. I didn't need my guy to be fancy, but when he looked that good in a tux, it was almost a crime not to wear one.

The vampire leaned down to whisper in my ear. "And you're as beautiful as Venus emerging from the sea."

"She was stark naked," I said.

He gave me devilish grin. "Perhaps wishful thinking on my part."

"Save your dirty thoughts for later," I said. "This wedding

is all about wholesome fun." No couple was more wholesome than Bentley and Meadow. The pair had met on the Magic-Mirror dating site and now here they were—ready to walk down the sandy aisle. It wouldn't surprise me in the least if the bride wore white flip-flips.

The groom hurried over when he spotted us. "Thank the gods. You're here."

"Of course we are," I said. "Wouldn't miss it for the world."

"And you're sure you're able to perform the spell?" Bentley asked. His cheeks and pointy ears were apple red and sweat bubbled on his forehead.

I clapped his narrow shoulder. "Chill out, Bentley. You just get yourself married and leave the magic to me."

He swallowed hard. "If you're certain…"

Alec shook his hand in an effort to relax the stressed elf. "Congratulations, Bentley. I have no doubt the ceremony will go off without a hitch."

"And even if it doesn't, that won't necessarily mean your marriage is doomed," a woman interjected. "Although I can't imagine meeting my spouse online. Seems like a recipe for disaster." She shuddered. "I'll never understand these younger generations with their questionable judgment."

"This is Shayna," Bentley said, clearly wishing Shayna was elsewhere right now. "She dates Meadow's uncle, Franco."

"We met the old-fashioned way," Shayna said. "He came into my shop and it was love at first sight."

"Which shop is that?" I asked.

"A resale shop over by Shining Stars and Charmed, I'm Sure," she said. "It's called Be-switched."

"Oh, I've seen that place," I said. "My daughter and I came in once because you had a softball glove in the window. It's not every day we see human world sports items here."

"Yes, I remember that one. Sold it to a collector for a tidy sum."

"Someone collects sports equipment from the human world?"

"You'd be surprised what buyers are interested in," Shayna said. "Just goes to show that money doesn't necessarily buy taste."

Soft music began to play. "That's my cue," Bentley said. He adjusted his bowtie. "How do I look?"

"Nervous. Try to breathe," I urged.

He made a few feeble attempts to breathe normally before he rushed to the gazebo.

"I guess you'd want pretentious music played at your wedding," I said.

Alec chuckled. "And what, pray tell, do you consider pretentious music?"

"Oh, I don't know. Dead white guy music." I smiled. "Basically you."

"And I suppose you'd want some sort of reggae or bongo beat to accompany us."

I recoiled. "Do you even know me?"

"I take it the reggae is a no." He patted his brow with a crisp, white handkerchief. "Good. I was fearful we'd have to end this right here and now."

"First of all, we'd have a Billy Joel cover band," I said. "Ours would be a sunset wedding because sunsets at the beach are awesome. Raoul would be the ring bearer. Wait, no. He'd probably pawn the rings for pizza. And Marley would be my maid of honor and you'd have..." I frowned. "Who would you have?"

He ignored my question. "Sounds like you've given this a lot of thought."

I shrugged. "Not really." Only when I accidentally watched a Hallmark movie from beginning to end, or skimmed the wedding announcements in *Vox Populi,* or heard a good slow song on the radio that we could claim as 'our song.'

Finally, it was our turn to be seated. "Bride or groom?" the usher asked.

"Groom," Alec said.

I poked his side. "Good thing you didn't wear your white linen suit or you might be mistaken for that guy," I whispered. I motioned to a werelynx in a seersucker suit and matching hat seated on the bride's side.

"I hardly think that's possible," he sniffed, and I laughed under my breath.

The usher escorted us to the second row on the groom's side. The row in front of us was comprised entirely of elves. I popped my head between two of them and said, "Hey, Smith family."

An elderly elf at the end of the row shushed me and I straightened.

Tanya fluttered down the row to sit beside me. "Wonderful day for a wedding, isn't it? You look lovely, Ember. That green is gorgeous on you."

"Matches your wings," I said. "Your dress is so pretty." The pale yellow dress seemed to capture the sunlight.

"Thank you," Tanya said. "I made it myself."

"I wish I had your talent," I said. "I can't even sew a button."

"That's what magic is for," the fairy replied. "Honestly, I don't understand why they waste your time with those lessons. Psychic skills and runecraft. What you need is good, old-fashioned home economics."

"I'll pass your thoughts to my aunt."

The music increased in volume and Alec slid his hand over mine. The ceremony wasn't too unlike a human one. Bentley and Meadow read vows they'd written themselves.

The officiant was a satyr named Xander who specialized in beach weddings and had undoubtedly earned his certification online. I spent half the ceremony wondering whether he'd get grains of sand caught in his hooves that would take weeks to dislodge.

"May the universe bestow its many gifts upon you," Xander said, concluding the ceremony. Apparently, that was the couple's cue to kiss. Bentley and Meadow nearly smacked foreheads but narrowly avoided a mishap. Everyone clapped politely. Not exactly a rowdy bunch.

"You're up," Tanya whispered and nudged me with her elbow.

Terrific. I stood and pointed my wand at the box on the ground next to the gazebo. If all went well, a hundred butterflies would burst out of the box and form the word 'love' above the couple's heads. I'd practiced at the cottage a handful of times without any issues, so I figured I had it in the bag.

Unfortunately, I was wrong.

Just as I cast the spell, a gust of wind blew past and knocked the tip of my wand to the left, where the spell hit a mosquito. Now, instead of one hundred beautiful butterflies in the air, there were one hundred mosquitoes. To make matters worse, the insects only managed to spell 'love' for a fraction of a second before they dropped dead and plummeted to the ground in a heap between the newly married couple. Bentley and Meadow jumped backward, releasing each other's hands and swatting at the falling mosquitoes.

"What an omen," someone shouted.

I waved my wand. "Not an omen! Just an act of nature!"

"Or an act of incompetence," someone else muttered.

Mother of pearl. I singlehandedly ruined Bentley's wedding with dead bugs. Slowly, I sat down and tucked away my wand. Alec offered a sympathetic smile and patted my knee.

"Please join us for a reception right here on Balefire Beach," Xander said quickly, and the guests sprang to their feet. I wasn't sure what the point of the stampede was. The mosquitoes were already dead.

"Maybe we should go," I said quietly to Alec.

"Since when do you allow embarrassment to guide your actions?" he asked.

"Bentley will want to strangle me."

"How is that different from any other day?" He smiled, showing his fangs. "Besides, I can't imagine you'd be willing to forgo an open bar on the beach. It's basically your dream date."

I looped my arm through his. "No, *you're* my dream date…on the beach with an open bar."

"Come along," he said. "I see a waiter with a tray full of bucksberry fizz."

"Just flash your fangs and take the whole tray," I urged. "He won't argue. We'll take our drinks and hide in a cove somewhere, so we don't have to mingle."

He laughed. "I'll do no such thing."

We merged with the other guests and ran into Shayna, the obnoxious troll. She had a colorful cocktail with flower petals floating on top.

"That looks amazing," I said. "Where can I get one of those?"

"The server with the unpolished horns who's currently making inappropriate small talk with that ghastly Tyra," she said. "You'd think she'd be better dressed for a wedding. After all, she calls herself a wardrobe designer. And, waiter or not, he really should have made himself more presentable. This isn't a car salesmen convention."

Meadow's uncle cleared his throat. "I understand you're in the newspaper business," Franco said. He directed his question to Alec, which was fair enough. Alec was the editor-in-chief and I was still trying to learn the ropes as a fledgling reporter.

"Lovely wedding," I said to Shayna. Small talk wasn't my favorite pastime, but I figured I'd make an effort for Bentley's sake. I only wished I could make an effort with someone more agreeable—or someone closer to the bar.

"It was fine," Shayna said dismissively. "Her dress looks like it was handed down one too many times, though. The cut was all wrong for her shape."

I was too startled to respond. While I wasn't the most polite individual on the planet, that seemed a bit much, even for me. I tried to change the direction of the conversation by complimenting her. I figured shifting the focus to her was the only way to stop her from making rude comments.

"That's a gorgeous brooch," I said. She wore a bejeweled pin in the shape of a flower affixed to her dress. Each petal was encrusted with a different colored gemstone.

"It is, isn't it? It once belonged to the famous socialite, Patricia Brickstone," Shayna said.

I shot Alec a helpless look. 'Paranormal famous' was like being 'Jersey pretty' as far as I was concerned.

"That's the upside of owning my own shop," she continued. "Items come in already used, so I'm able to use them myself before I resell them without feeling the least bit guilty. I once wore a wrap to the opera that belonged to Madame Kasov. I still sold it the next day for a fantastic price. That money went directly into my vacation fund."

I'd never heard of Madame Kasov either, but I offered a vague smile. "Cool," was the only word that seemed to capable of leaving my mouth.

To my relief, we were interrupted by Bentley's slightly inebriated aunt and uncle.

"So when will it be your turn?" Bentley's aunt asked me.

"Bentley says the two of you are so in love that he keeps an anti-nausea potion in his desk drawer."

"Gladys!" her husband admonished her. "You're not supposed to repeat things like that."

I avoided Alec's gaze. "We're not in a rush. It's early days."

"Naturally, he's not in a rush," Gladys agreed. "He's an immortal vampire. You, my dear, have an expiration date." A server passed by with a tray of drinks and she swapped her empty glass for a full one.

"Let them move at their own pace," her husband said. "If we'd have waited, we probably wouldn't be married now."

"Vito, that's a horrible thing to say." She sucked down the booze like it was her last drink before stepping up to the guillotine.

"She's quite right," Shayna said. "I'm not interested in children—far too messy—so I never felt marriage was a priority, but from the looks of you, you're running out of time."

I bristled.

"Now, Shayna," Franco said, sensing my annoyance. "Ember doesn't look a day over…child-bearing age." He wisely opted not to step into the field of land mines.

"Alec and I are happy as we are," I said. I didn't want to get into personal information. It wasn't their business. And Alec would be mortified to share details of our relationship with relative strangers. He had a hard enough time talking in therapy. At least he was still willing to partake. I'd worried that he would bail when it became too uncomfortable for him. So far, though, he seemed committed.

"Meadow, sweetie." Gladys lost interest in us and waved to the blushing bride.

"Congratulations," I said, as she approached us. Meadow seemed to have shaken off the awkwardness of the ceremony and was radiating with pure joy. If I could have bottled her positive energy and dabbed it behind my ears every morning for the rest of my life, I would have.

"Where are you off to for this honeymoon of yours?" Franco asked. "I heard something about Africa."

"Oh, you wouldn't want to go there this time of year," Shayna said. "They're in the Southern Hemisphere."

"Shayna is well traveled," Franco said, somewhat apologetically.

I was relieved when the troll gave Franco a quick kiss on the cheek and disappeared into the crowd.

"Knowing Bentley, he voted for a staycation," I said.

Meadow giggled. "He is somewhat of a homebody, but I don't mind."

My eyes popped. "Oh no. You're not actually doing that, are you?" I'd have to box those pointy ears of his if he'd persuaded his blushing bride to go *nowhere* for their honeymoon.

"We settled on a cruise," Meadow said. "We leave early tomorrow." She turned to face Alec. "Thank you for arranging it, by the way. It's a really generous gift."

I cut a quick glance at Alec. He hadn't told me that he paid for their honeymoon. Every time I thought the vampire couldn't surprise me anymore, he found a way.

"Enjoy your time together," Alec said. "Make it one of your most cherished memories."

"Today is already on the list," Meadow said with a contented sigh. "Everyone thinks weddings are all about the bride and groom, but it's really about the loved ones connected to us. Together, we form a complete circle, like my wedding band." She played with the new ring on her finger.

"That's sweet, Meadow," I said. "How many drinks have you had anyway?"

Bentley appeared between us, struggling to undo his bowtie. "Formalwear at the beach. Whose idea was this?"

"Keep going with those buttons and it's officially a party," I declared.

"Now who's had too much to drink?" Meadow teased.

I raised my hand. "I'm sorry about the dead bugs."

Bentley chuckled. "It's fine, Ember. You added a memorable moment for our guests."

Alec slipped an arm around my waist. "Ember is full of memorable moments. One of the many reasons that our time together is so special."

"Really?" My head swiveled to look at him. "How special?"

His eyes twinkled like two stars and, for a moment, I was mesmerized. "In my long life, I've never wanted to know anyone the way I want to know you."

Bentley groaned. "Please stop. I don't have my anti-nausea potion on me."

"I think it's wonderful," Meadow said. "The world needs more happy couples."

My heart thumped so hard that I was pretty sure it shook my bladder. Or—again—maybe it was down to the multiple glasses of bucksberry fizz. Who could say with certainty? Whatever the cause, now I was in dire need of the bathroom. It hadn't occurred to me that we were on the beach with no indoor plumbing. I jostled Meadow's arm.

"Bathroom," I squeaked. If too many syllables leaked out of my mouth, there was a risk that another leak would follow.

She pointed at a row of portable toilets set up further down the beach. I kicked off my shoes and hurried toward them like an oasis in the desert.

"All the magic in this town and they still have port-a-potties?" I muttered.

Each one I tried was locked or out of toilet paper, so I continued down the row until I reached the one on the end. The door seemed more stuck than locked, so I gave it a yank.

Finally, the door swung open and, before I could enter, a large paranormal toppled forward. I stumbled backward to avoid her and fell flat in the sand. The guest landed on top of me with a thud.

"I'm so sorry," I said, struggling to breathe with her weight on me. "Are you okay?"

She didn't move and I wondered whether she'd been knocked unconscious. I managed to roll her off of me and realized with a start that the guest was Shayna. I wiggled her arm and called her name but to no avail. Panic erupted inside me.

A guest emerged from the neighboring stall. "Someone's had too many drinks," the berserker said and laughed.

"No," I said, a wave of nausea washing over me. My dream wedding had suddenly become a nightmare. "Someone's dead."

CHAPTER THREE

"You can't be serious, Rose." Deputy Bolan looked from me to the dead troll on the beach. "You're like a walking reminder of the circle of life. I'm glad you weren't at my wedding. I probably wouldn't have made it out alive."

I glared at the leprechaun. "It was an accident."

"No, an accident is not making it to the toilet in time," the deputy said, smirking.

A blush rose to my cheeks. Thankfully, I'd dashed into the empty stall the berserker had vacated while I waited for the sheriff and deputy to arrive.

"Now, Deputy. Let's keep this investigation about the deceased." Sheriff Granger Nash swaggered his way around the troll's body. "Why don't we clear the area and secure the scene?"

"Everybody, go back to your libations," the deputy shouted.

"You can't close off the whole area," I said. "We need at least one toilet. There are about a hundred guests here."

"I see where your priorities are, Rose," Deputy Bolan said.

The sheriff gave me a lingering look before turning to the deputy. "Leave the stall at the far end available for guests, please. We're not animals." He paused. "Most of the time."

"Got it," the leprechaun replied.

Loitering guests shuffled back to the reception, except one who came storming through the crowd. *Crap in a burrito.* Franco took one look at the lifeless body in the sand and rushed forward.

"Shayna?" He shook her shoulders. "Shayna, what happened?"

"Sir, I'm going to have to ask you to take a step back," Sheriff Nash said.

Franco's expression crumpled. "Is she going to be okay? Where are the healers?"

I crouched beside him. "Franco," I said softly. "Why don't you come with me? Your son's here, isn't he?"

"Right here," the young man said. I'd met him earlier but had already forgotten his name. He looked nothing like Franco, so I assumed he favored his mother. According to Bentley, Meadow's aunt had died a few years ago when their son was away at university.

"I'm Sheriff Nash," the werewolf said. "Would you mind taking your dad home for now? We'll want to speak with him, but we've got work to do first."

"Of course," the young man said. I moved aside so that he could coax his dad away from Shayna. "Dad, I'm going to take you home now, okay?"

Franco wrapped his arms around his girlfriend and started to sob. "Why does this keep happening to me?"

He placed a gentle hand on his father's shoulder. "Come on, Dad. Let the police do their work."

"I'm sorry for your loss," I said, as Franco's son managed to steer him away. I turned back to the sheriff. "I guess you want me to go, too."

"Never, Rose," he replied, so quietly that I almost didn't hear him. Almost. He cleared his throat. "As long as you don't get underfoot, you can stay."

"Sheriff," the leprechaun started to complain but quickly clamped his mouth shut. He knew better to argue with his boss when it came to me.

"It looks like she choked to death," the sheriff said. "There's evidence of vomiting in the stall."

"It's a wedding," I said. "That could be anyone's." Thankfully, my dizzy head was slowly clearing. A dead troll will sober anyone up quickly.

"I'll be sure to have it tested, Rose," he said. "This isn't my first crime scene."

"Sorry," I mumbled. "I know you know what you're doing."

He cupped a hand to his ear. "What was that? I don't think I heard you."

"Hey, boss," the deputy said. "Did you see her neck?"

"I'm not here to ogle Rose, Deputy," he replied. "Besides, it's not her neck I'm most interested in. I'm not Hale, am I?"

I brushed off the remark. I knew that Granger was still hurting so it was no surprise that he'd take a potshot at Alec.

"Not *her* neck," the leprechaun said. "Hers." He pointed to the troll.

Sheriff Nash seemed mildly embarrassed by the misunderstanding. "Yeah. Red marks. Evidence of a struggle."

"Not an accident, Rose," the deputy said, not bothering to disguise his smug tone.

"You're celebrating the fact that someone's been murdered and at a wedding no less?" I clucked my tongue. "For shame, Deputy."

Alec appeared in the distance. I could tell that he was reluctant to come any closer and endure one of the sheriff's inevitable scowls.

"Looks like the reception is clearing out anyway," I said. "I think word got around."

"Deputy, prepare the victim for transport," the sheriff said.

"Do you need help with anything?" I asked. "I don't have upper body strength, but I have a wand."

"Yeah, I heard about your wand action during the ceremony," the deputy said with a snicker. "I passed guests talking about it on the way across the beach."

"They spelled love," I said, determined not to let the leprechaun ruffle my feathers. "Butterflies, mosquitoes. What's the difference?"

"You did go to school in New Jersey, didn't you?" Deputy Bolan asked. "Or did you spend all your time at Bon Jovi concerts?"

I gasped. "Bite your tongue, little man. I wouldn't be caught dead at a Bon Jovi concert."

"Can you two quit your bickering for five minutes so we can finish up here?"

I looked at the sheriff askance, but he wasn't looking at me. I realized that he'd spotted Alec lingering in the distance. Waiting for me. Ugh.

"You know what? I should go," I said. "I'm getting in the way."

"Wow, a moment of introspection. Write this day down in your diary."

I glared at the leprechaun before exiting the crime scene. "I'll see you guys around."

"Goodnight, Rose," the sheriff said. "That shade of green suits you. You should wear it more often."

"Thanks." I walked along the beach toward Alec, conscious of the sheriff's gaze burning a hole in my back. The vampire extended a hand as I approached.

"It's been quite the evening," he said.

"I've had worse," I said.

As we started toward the parking lot, I spotted Franco. He sat alone on the beach, staring blankly at the rolling waves. All evidence of the wedding had been cleared away and his son was nowhere to be found. I'd clearly been at the crime scene longer than I'd realized.

"Give me a minute," I whispered to Alec. I walked over and joined Franco on the sand. "You didn't go home."

"How could I?" he asked. "My life is still on the beach." He glanced over to the secured area where his girlfriend's body had been. "She's gone?"

"They took her body to be examined," I said. "You want to find out what happened, don't you?"

He wiped his nose with his sleeve. "Of course."

"Can you think of any reason someone would want to hurt her?" I asked.

He snapped to attention. "You think she was murdered?" The color drained from his face. "I thought it was a medical issue, or she hit her head and fell. Great Goddess. This is even worse."

"There were marks on her neck that suggest she may have been strangled," I said. "The sheriff will know more after the body's been examined."

"Strangled?" Franco covered his face with his hands. "I mean, she wasn't always easy to get along with. She was tough, but to kill her?" He started to cry again. "Why am I talking about her in the past tense? Stars and stones, this is awful."

"I'm so sorry," I said. "I can't imagine what you're going through right now."

"Can we drive you home?" Alec asked, emerging from the shadows. "I have a driver here."

"Thanks, but I'll be fine," he said. "I can walk from here. It's not that far."

"Are you sure?" I asked. I hated to leave him but could understand wanting time alone to process the day's seismic events.

"My son's waiting for me at home," Franco said. "I told him I'd be there soon."

Alec clasped my hand. "Terribly sorry about Shayna. I only met her briefly, but she seemed like a wonderfully strong woman."

Wonderfully strong. That was one way to describe her. No wonder Alec was a writer.

"I never imagined myself with a troll, to be honest. I always dated petite women before her, but there was something about Shayna that grabbed me from our first meeting, you know?"

Alec's gaze flickered to me. "I do know."

"She said it was love at first sight and I don't know if it was that instant for me, but it was pretty darn close." He pressed his forehead to his knees. "I thought I was safe after my first wife, that I couldn't lose another one. Life doesn't notice how much has already been taken from you, though. There's no checks and balances."

"No, I'm afraid there isn't," Alec said. "Ask any vampire and they'll all say the same."

Franco's head bobbed up and down. "On the one hand, it's depressing but also sort of encouraging, you know?"

I squeezed his shoulder. "Take care, Franco," I said, and walked to the car with Alec.

"Not exactly the wedding they hoped for, was it?" Alec asked, once we were safely installed in the backseat. "Bentley likely wishes that the dead mosquitoes were, indeed, the highlight."

"I'd give him a thousand dead bugs if I thought it would help."

"Guests kept murmuring about bad omens," Alec said. "That the marriage is doomed."

"A wedding isn't a marriage," I said matter-of-factly. "I have no doubt that Meadow and Bentley will be fine."

"We're doing crafts again today?" I complained. I still felt mildly nauseous from the events of yesterday's wedding. I wasn't really in the mood for lessons.

The Master of Ritual Toolcraft frowned at me. "We do not do *crafts*, Ember. These are essential tools in support of the craft."

"Right. So crafts."

He gave an impatient sigh. "Craft as in short for witchcraft and wizardry. Not crafts like popsicle sticks and glue."

"There's also the cheese," I said. "Kraft."

He closed his eyes and I knew he was likely counting to ten in his head. I'd done it enough times with Raoul to recognize the expression. "I'm not familiar with any cheese by that name."

"That's because you've never had yellow squares of it each individually wrapped in a plastic. Now doesn't that sound delicious?"

Lee stared at me for a beat and then set his bag on the table. "Tell me, Ember. When the troll fell on top of you yesterday, did you hit your head on the ground? Maybe suffered a concussion?"

"No, the sand cushioned the blow."

"You might want to get a healer's opinion on that." He unzipped the compartment and produced a work in progress.

"You're a wizard," I said. "You should really think about

carrying stuff around in something more magical than a carry-on suitcase."

He continued to retrieve items from the bag and set them neatly on the dining table. "This is not a suitcase, Ember. This is a bag designed to transport items from place to place. The handle and wheels simply make it easier to move."

"So it's a suitcase." I picked up a pair of shears and began snapping them open and closed as though they were the mouth of an alligator. He snatched them from me and set them on his side of the table.

"We're going to resume work on your Book of Shadows today."

"I guess I'm okay with that," I said. "It's not too mentally taxing. At least Marigold isn't here. I wouldn't be able to handle her energy level today." The Mistress of Psychic Skills was a cross between a cheerleader and a drill sergeant.

"Would you rather I trade ritual toolcraft for an afternoon of opera with the coven bard?"

I shivered. "Why would you even suggest such a thing?"

Lee chuckled. "I thought that might be your reaction. Now, which color ribbon would you like to use. We'll attach it to the interior spine so that you can use it as a bookmark. The best way to avoid those wretched dog-eared pages is to have a built-in marker like this."

"Good goddess," I said. "Marley is going to pee her pants when it's time to make her own Book of Shadows."

Lee scrunched his nose. "You say that like it's a good thing."

"I just realized that both Book of Shadows and Big Book of Scribbles have the same abbreviation—BOS." I paused. "No, wait. I guess the other one is technically BBOS." I shrugged. "Close enough."

Lee fell silent.

"You're counting in your head again, aren't you?" I asked.

"It's not counting." He forced a smile. "Anyhoo, I've brought an assortment of embellishments that you may want to consider for both the exterior and interior of the book."

I peered into the suitcase to see a collection of small shiny objects. "You know? I'm in the mood for a little bedazzlement. I saw a really pretty pin at the wedding yesterday with all these tiny gemstones..." I stopped talking when I realized that I'd seen the pin on Shayna. "You know what? Never mind. Let's make it all gray and black so it's gloomy."

"Your Book of Shadows should reflect you, Ember," Lee said.

"What are you trying to say? That you don't think I'm gloomy doomy? Lee, I think that's the nicest vague compliment you've ever given me."

"I only mean to say that if you would like this book to be a happy, safe place for you, then treat it as such. If the sight of dazzling stones along the edge of the book will perk you up, then by all means, be this book's glam squad."

I shot him a curious look. "Lee, have you been dipping into episodes of Real Housewives on Bravo?"

Lee maintained a neutral expression. "I have no idea what you're talking about. Must be a human world thing."

I wore a vague smile. "Must be."

His gaze shifted to the corner of the room and his brow furrowed. "I hate to ask, but what is that thing?"

I realized he was pointing to the scratching post. "Oh, that was a gift from Raoul to Bonkers. He won it at the dump."

"There are no winners if that's in your house."

"They dig their claws into it," I explained. "It's relaxing or something. Don't worry. I won't make you test it out."

"Can you at least change the color? It's ghastly."

I studied the strange shade of green. "I guess I can use

magic. I hadn't really thought about it." Using magic still wasn't second nature to me.

"I'm happy to do it for you," Lee offered. "Name a color. Any color. As long as it isn't that one."

"How about rainbow stripes?" I asked. Marley was a big fan.

Lee pursed his lips, probably regretting his open-ended offer. "As you wish." He took out his wand and aimed it at the scratching post.

"You know what?" I interrupted. "If you can tolerate it this one time, I think I'd like to let Marley do the honors. She's been practicing color spells, so it would be good for her."

Lee tucked his wand away. "Fair enough. I'll avert my eyes."

"How do you think I get through my lessons with Hazel?"

He stifled a laugh. "I am sorry about what happened to you yesterday. It must have been a terrible shock."

"Not as terrible as what happened to Shayna." I pictured the troll's lifeless body on the ground. "I got off easy."

"I hope the sheriff is able to apprehend the killer quickly," Lee said.

"I'm sure he will," I said. "Sheriff Nash is devoted to his job."

"Yes, this town has been lucky to have him," Lee said, "though I know your aunt might disagree. Then again, she'd only be happy if she wore the star badge."

I laughed. "What are you trying to say, Lee? That my aunt is a control freak?"

"I wouldn't dream of it."

"Just out of curiosity, have you ever seen her Book of Shadows?" I asked.

"Of course not. Why would you think that?"

"Because you're the expert," I said.

"Not when it comes to your aunt," he said. "Hyacinth Rose-Muldoon is the expert unless explicitly stated otherwise."

I began plucking out colorful bling for my book. "I don't know how my cousins aren't more messed up. They should be train wreck city."

"They were fortunate to have other influences, like their father."

"What was he like?" I asked. I couldn't imagine the man brave enough to put a ring on her finger. It was one thing to date her like Craig and Zale, but another thing to pledge to live the rest of your life with her. An early death seemed like the only sensible option.

"A very practical, very even-tempered wizard," Lee said. "He was a respected member of the coven and the community."

"He'd have to be to meet my aunt's exacting standards." I glued a few beads on the cover. "Was he a good dad?"

"Muldoon was involved," Lee said. "Took Linnea and Aster to their dance lessons and Florian to whatever activity of the week he'd decided to try and then abandon."

"That hasn't changed," I said.

"Florian was always a wayward wizard," Lee admitted. "I think we all thought he'd find his footing once his father died, but it didn't happen."

"Because his mother coddles him," I said. Not that Florian was a bad guy. He wasn't. He'd proven to be a great friend to me and took a genuine interest in Marley, which I appreciated. He seemed content to coast through life, though. No ambition. No relationship goals. I worried that he'd end up in his mother's basement forever. Granted, the basement of Thornhold was basically a mini-mansion, but still.

"And you don't coddle Marley?" Lee asked. Amusement danced in his dark eyes.

"What? No!" I thought about Marley sleeping in bed and eating whatever she wanted. "Okay, maybe a little, but only a normal amount."

"I see."

"What do you think of Hyacinth getting her dating groove on?" I asked. "Is it weird for the coven to see her acting like she has the same organs as the rest of us?"

Lee snipped a section of ribbon and handed it to me. "It's certainly unexpected, but she seems to be in good spirits as a result. That's a win for the coven."

"I really like Zale, but that wizard's been skulking around, too," I said.

"Linden's cousin, isn't he?" Lee asked.

"Yes. I've seen their car at the main house a couple of times recently." In fact, Marley and I had been invited to join them for drinks and nibbles tomorrow, which seemed to be a statement. My aunt didn't tend to mix family members and 'others' for social gatherings unless it meant something.

"Hyacinth has always been partial to intercoven relationships."

"True. I think he's probably more her type in the long-term anyway. He's way more polished than Zale." The absence of fins was a plus, too.

"Yes, your aunt does prize certain qualities above others, as do we all."

"And which qualities do you prize, Lee?"

He appeared thoughtful. "The ability to work in companionable silence."

"That's highly specific."

He gave me a pointed look. "And not a very good hint, apparently."

It took me a moment, but I eventually caught on. "Fine, Master of Solitude. I'll be quiet. Seems boring though. Why work in silence when you have the opportunity to chat with me? What if you miss out on the answers to life's big questions because you wanted to work in 'companionable silence?'"

He heaved an exaggerated sigh. "It's a risk, Ember, but I suppose it's a chance I'll just have to take."

CHAPTER FOUR

I WASN'T sure what the appropriate attire was for drinks and nibbles with my aunt's prospective suitor, so I settled on a sundress with strappy sandals that Florian had dubbed 'lazy chic.' The ensemble received Marley's stamp of approval, which was really all I needed.

"Do you want to ride Firefly over?" I asked. Aunt Hyacinth had given the beloved unicorn to Marley as a gift.

Marley chewed her lip. "That just seems like showing off."

"I know. I thought I might give Aunt Hyacinth the chance to preen a little for Craig's benefit. I was throwing her a bone."

Marley smiled as she ran a brush through her dark hair. "You think she likes him?"

"You've seen Linden's car parked in the driveway as much as I have. They may as well embroider the napkins now."

"Can Bonkers come?"

I glanced to the scratching post where the flying kitten was keeping herself occupied. "I think she'll be happier here."

"You're not going to really make me change the color, are you?" Marley asked. I'd mentioned Lee's comment to her. I tried to spin it as the chance to practice her magic, but she didn't bite.

"Not if you prefer it the way it is."

Marley wrinkled her nose. "It is ugly, but I don't want to hurt Raoul's feelings. Besides, Bonkers doesn't mind the color."

Inwardly, I sighed. How could I argue with her compassionate logic?

We left the cottage and enjoyed the long albeit lovely walk to the main house. Craig Buckley-Croft was already on the veranda, along with his cousin, Linden Buckley-Clay. Linden was a member of the local coven who'd been away for almost a year. She'd returned after her mother's recent passing with her handsome cousin in tow. The attractive cousins were close in age—probably mid-fifties—and shared similar features, including a patrician nose and cinnamon-colored hair.

"I'd like to introduce you both to my daughter, Marley," I said.

"One of the newest members of the coven," Linden said, giving Marley a cheerful smile. "How exciting."

"A pleasure to see you again, Ember," Craig said. "Your aunt was kind enough to invite us yet again. This house is a true wonder."

"And Simon is an absolute treasure," Linden said. "I hope Hyacinth realizes how fortunate she is to have good help."

As challenging as my aunt could be, I knew how much she valued her staff, especially Simon. "Oh, we all worship Simon," I said.

"I understand you occupy that sweet cottage at the back of the property," Craig said.

"Yes, Rose Cottage belonged to my parents," I said.

"How fascinating that your aunt secured the main house

while your father was relegated to the cottage," Craig mused. "I suppose there's a story there."

"Yes, the story is that my aunt always gets her way," I said. It bothered me that Craig seemed acutely aware of the grandeur. I suddenly flashed back to the coven meeting where we first met—how enthralled he was by our impressive headquarters and the fact that the Roses were descendants of the One True Witch. It occurred to me that he might actually be more interested in prestige than in my aunt.

On cue, Aunt Hyacinth swept onto the veranda, looking resplendent in a white kaftan trimmed in gold. Her white-blond hair was pulled in a tight chignon and two of the fingers on her right hand sported gold bands. Although my aunt was always dressed for an impromptu audience with the queen, she'd clearly taken extra care with her appearance today. Interesting.

"I do apologize for keeping you waiting," my aunt said. She greeted Linden with a kiss on each cheek and shook Craig's hand with a limp wrist. "Florian should be joining us any moment. We were delayed by a meeting."

My radar pinged. "What kind of meeting? Not the foundation?"

"No, darling," my aunt said. "I was assisting him with a tourism matter. Sometimes a voice of authority is needed." She shifted her attention back to her guests. "Has Simon taken care of you?"

"He tried, but we told him we'd wait for you," Linden said.

"You're too kind," Aunt Hyacinth said. She pulled one of her omnipresent bells from the deep recesses of her kaftan. Before she managed to ring it, Simon appeared with a tray of drinks.

"Oh, how clever he is," Linden said.

"They have a psychic bond," I said. They really didn't, but it sure seemed that way most of the time.

"I took the liberty of preparing gentian spritzes," Aunt Hyacinth said.

"One of my absolute favorites," Linden exclaimed.

"Our grandmother used to make these at holidays," Craig added.

"Yes, you mentioned that last week," my aunt said.

Wait, what? Craig made a personal comment and my aunt tucked that nugget away for later use? To be *thoughtful*? What sorcery was this?

They each plucked a glass from the tray. Marley gave me a hopeful look, but I shook my head. Linden took an excited sip and nearly splashed it down her front.

"Silly me," Linden said. "I'm far too eager to let my taste buds stroll down memory lane."

"Perfect timing," Florian said, rounding the corner of the exterior of the house. "I do love showing up as the drinks are served. Pleased to see it isn't tea. I thought I'd have to sneak a spell to spruce mine up."

"The weather is so pleasant," my aunt said. "I decided that the spritzes were better suited to the temperature."

"Your instincts are spot on as always, Hyacinth," Craig said. He tasted more of his spritzer. "This really brings back happy memories, doesn't it, Linden?"

"Do you remember how our grandparents would play the piano side by side?" She sighed at the memory. "He would play on the left and she would play on the right. What wonderful music they made together."

"They're the reason we're both single," Craig admitted. "It's hard to measure up to a relationship like the one they had. I've been too intimidated to try."

"Same," Linden agreed. "And once Mother became ill, I couldn't focus on much else anyway."

"I understand," I said. "When my husband died, I became

fixated on my daughter. I didn't make time for anything except earning a living and taking care of her."

"That's a good mother," Craig said. "Dreadful about your husband."

"Thank you," I said.

"Ember's currently dating Alec Hale," my aunt announced.

"Alec Hale?" Linden repeated. "The vampire?"

I nodded.

"How fascinating," Linden said. She took another drink.

"Mother's mellowed since Ember arrived in town," Florian said. He'd already polished off his drink. "She's not the coven hardliner she used to be."

Aunt Hyacinth pinched his cheek. "You wish."

"You're her son and heir," Craig said. "Her concern is understandable."

"Presumably you're a son and heir," I said.

Craig's expression clouded over. "Naturally. At my age, you can imagine the disappointment in my parents' eyes every time they see me."

I smacked Florian's arm. "Study this guy. He's your Ghost of Christmas Future."

Marley laughed. As I turned to put my glass on an end table, I caught sight of a familiar leprechaun lurking on the edge of the lawn. "Excuse me, I'll be right back." I hurried across the grass to meet him. "What's up, Little Hulk?"

He didn't seem happy to be here. "Sorry to interrupt your rich folks family gathering, but I need to talk to you."

I frowned. "Is this about Shayna?"

"No, it's worse."

"Worse than a dead wedding guest?" Yikes. I almost didn't want to hear what he had to say.

The leprechaun swore under his breath. "Dear gods, I

hate to resort to this, but I'm desperate. Sheriff Nash is behaving…oddly."

"Oddly how?"

He scratched the back of his head. "How should I put this? He's behaving like a…like Wyatt."

The Nash brothers couldn't be further apart in personality. Where Granger was respectful and compassionate, Wyatt was a giant dung beetle.

"Did something happen?" I asked. "Maybe he hit his head?"

"And it accidentally switched him into jerk mode?' the deputy asked, exasperated. "He's not a toy. This has to be something else."

"You think someone put a spell on him?" It was possible. This was Starry Hollow, after all.

"I don't know," he said. "I mean, if you're going to cast a spell on the sheriff, why would you make him…Wyatt?"

"I guess it depends on what your motivation is," I said. "Are you sure he's really acting out of character and not having a bad day or something?"

The leprechaun's beady eyes fixed on me. "He's at the Wishing Well right now. Why don't you go check him out and let me know if you think he's just having a bad day?"

A knot formed in my stomach. "Okay, I guess I can take a quick ride over there."

The deputy zigzagged a finger in front of my outfit. "You might want to change before you go."

I looked down at my clothes. "What's wrong with this?" If it passed muster with Aunt Hyacinth, how could it not be appropriate for the Wishing Well?

"It's a cute sundress, Rose," the deputy said. "I don't even play on your team and I can tell you that hits all the right notes with my gender." He motioned in the direction of the cottage. "Go put on those baggy jeans you find so comfortable and a plaid shirt. The one that makes you look like a lumberjack."

I squinted at him. "Are you sure Granger is the one with the issue right now?"

His nostrils flared. "Trust me. I wouldn't be coming to you if I weren't concerned and I certainly wouldn't subject the sheriff to you unnecessarily."

I glared at him. "What's that supposed to mean—subject the sheriff to me?"

"Come on, Rose. You know exactly what I mean. I want him to get over you and that means the less interaction, the better. You need to stop showing up when there's a dead body. You're like some kind of corpse psychic."

"Corpse psychic?" Florian interjected. "I'd watch that show."

"Where did you come from?" I asked.

"I was trying to eavesdrop from the veranda but it was too difficult, so I just decided to walk over."

"I have to go," I said. "Aunt Hyacinth won't mind, will she?"

Florian snorted. "I don't think she'd notice if we all vacated the premises. As long as Craig is there, we're all just background noise."

"Your aunt has another new beau?" Deputy Bolan asked. "Isn't this her third in recent memory?"

"So what? She's emerged from the relationship desert and my girl is *thirsty*," I said. I cast a sidelong glance at Florian. "Now I know where you get it, by the way." All this time I assumed that my cousin's flirtatious ways were inherited from the Muldoon side of the family, but Aunt Hyacinth's recent behavior had changed my opinion.

"Can I come with you?" Florian asked.

"I'm not planning to stay. I only want to help the deputy

with an issue. Can you do me a favor and hang out with Marley until I get back?"

Florian glanced back at the veranda where Marley was patiently listening to Craig blather on about…well, probably the stock market and whether it's a bull or a bear market right now.

"Okay, fine," he said. "I can't leave her in the lurch like that. It would be cruel and unusual punishment."

"Thanks, you're the best." I turned to the leprechaun. "We'll take my car so I don't have to adjust the seat."

The deputy pointed toward the cottage. "You'll take your car because I'm not coming with you."

"Why not?"

He waved his hands in front of him. "No way. If he figures out I sent you there, I'll be on his list."

"He keeps a list?" I could picture Aunt Hyacinth keeping a list of perceived slights, but not Sheriff Nash.

"You're on your own, Rose," he said, and scuttled back to his car.

"You sure you don't want a wingman?" Florian asked.

I patted his chest. "Not today, Goose. I'm afraid I've got to take the highway to the danger zone all by myself."

The darkened interior of the Wishing Well made it difficult to find the sheriff until my eyesight adjusted. I stood in the entryway and blinked a few times until his familiar silhouette came into view.

At first glance, I thought he was Wyatt. He was clearly making smooth moves on a pixie at the bar and she seemed to be totally on board with his suggestion.

I approached with caution. "Granger?"

The sheriff turned from his companion, his hand still on her thigh. "Oh, hey there. Didn't expect to see you here tonight. Shouldn't you be snuggling in front of a warm fire with that cold-blooded vamp of yours?"

The pixie giggled. "Get it? Because he's dead, so he's cold."

I ignored her and focused on Granger. "What's going on?"

He cocked his head. "You say that in a tone that suggests something shouldn't be going on. Last time I checked, that was no longer your business."

"You two used to date?" The pixie looked from the sheriff to me. "Huh. I never would've guessed."

My hands moved to my hips. "Why not?"

The pixie shrugged. "You don't seem like his type."

I fought the urge to clap back. This wasn't about me. This was about Granger's behavior.

The sheriff must have sensed my inner struggle because a lazy grin emerged and he slung an arm around my shoulders. "Ladies, ladies. There's more than enough of The Big G to go around. I'm a wolf, remember? Your needs are my needs." He winked at the pixie.

"Can I talk to you alone for a minute?" I asked.

"As long as we're only going to talk," he said, nodding his head toward the pixie. "First come, first served." He scratched the scruff along his jawline. "I guess it should be first served, first come." He laughed.

I grabbed him by the back of his collar and tugged him toward a dark corner of the room.

"Ooh, it's cozy here. I like where your head's at, gorgeous," he said. "Never could resist a pretty sundress." He snaked an arm around my waist and I swatted it away.

"What's gotten into you?" I demanded.

"You," he said. "And Bessie over there." He turned to wave at her. "And I like the looks of that blonde on the stool, too. Nice legs."

Deputy Bolan was right. This was not the Granger I knew.

"I'd like to know how the investigation is coming along," I said. Maybe I could get him to talk to me in sheriff mode.

The werewolf inched closer to me. "Why don't you come back to my office where it's nice and private and we'll look over the notes together?"

"Granger, stop. Just be normal for a hot minute."

He spread his arms wide. "This *is* normal, honeypot. I'm a Nash. This is who we are."

My nose scrunched. "Honeypot? You always call me Rose."

"I'm more than willing to call you anything you like." He squeezed my butt and I pulled away, my temper flaring.

"You know what? Forget it. Whatever's going on with you, you're on your own."

"Fine by me. That's the way I like it anyway. Lone wolf stalking his prey." He sauntered back to Bessie, leaving me alone in the corner of the bar.

"Wow, that was brutal," a voice said.

I shifted to a shadowy figure huddled in the corner booth. "Deputy! I thought you weren't coming."

"I wanted to see if his behavior changed when you were alone. He couldn't know I was here."

"Well, he failed your test. Or passed. Whatever." I groaned. "If this keeps up, it's going to be a mess." The Starry Hollow sheriff couldn't run around town acting like a womanizing fool. One Wyatt Nash was enough for the whole town and, thankfully, he wasn't in a position of authority.

The deputy blew out a breath. "Yeah, the question is— what do I do about it?"

"How far into the investigation are you?" I asked.

"We spoke to Franco and Brad," he began.

I snapped my fingers. "Brad! Why can't I remember that kid's name?"

"Because you're too self-involved?"

I ignored him. "And you ruled them out?"

"Yeah. No motives and neither one had ventured over to the toilets during the wedding. There are witnesses to vouch for them the whole time, but Mr. Lothario has been too busy chasing tail to chase leads."

"And we've got a murderer on the loose."

"That we do."

I slumped in the chair across from him. "You blame me for this, don't you?"

The leprechaun didn't meet my gaze. "I'm not interested in blame, Rose. I'm interested in helping my friend."

I cast a glance over my shoulder to see Granger smacking lips with the pixie. Although I wanted him to be happy, I knew this wasn't the way.

"The only thing I can recommend right now is a cold shower."

"Tried that last night," the deputy said. "Ended up wrestling a wolf on a wet bathroom floor. Trust me. Not as sexy as it sounds."

"Hopefully it's a phase and he'll snap out of it quickly," I said, not sure whether I truly believed it.

He cut a glance at the bar sign. "This is the Wishing Well. I guess I'll toss in a coin and see if that does the trick." He observed the sheriff for another uncomfortable moment. "Do me a favor and make sure none of this ends up in the paper. I don't want a permanent record of this."

"It's *Vox Populi* not Radar Online. We don't use the word canoodling."

"I think I can guess where his noodle is ending up tonight."

I cringed. "A pox upon your house for that visual."

"It bothers you, doesn't it?" he asked.

"It bothers you, too. Why else did you drag me down here?"

Deputy Bolan fixed me with a hard stare. "You know what I mean."

I rose to my feet. "I gave up the right to be bothered in that way. I have no claim on him."

"You do when you're still walking around with his heart, Rose."

My chest squeezed. "Good luck with the investigation, Deputy. I hope he comes to his senses soon." I left the bar without a backward glance and hurried to my car, wanting to put distance between us. If Granger wanted to sow his wild oats, it wasn't my place to whack him with a rake. As tempted as I was to help, Granger was going to have to work through this one on his own.

CHAPTER FIVE

"Is that your ancestor's grimoire?" Alec asked as he stood and stretched. He'd been on the sofa in the cottage, working on the edits for his latest book while I poked through the grimoire at the table. I was feeling uncharacteristically proud of myself because I'd managed to use Calla's *Illumináre* spell to read the contents in English.

"Yes, I've been trying to see if there are any clues."

"Clues to what?" He leaned down and nuzzled the side of my neck.

"To her. To what happened. Like, why does her wand feel like it was crafted with the tears of puppies and lost toys?"

He sat beside me and looked at the grimoire. "This is simply a book of spells, Ember. It doesn't seem to include anything of a personal nature."

"No, I'd need her Book of Shadows for that, but we have to work with what we've got." I flipped the page and the title of the next spell caught my eye. "Hmm. This has potential."

He inched closer and I felt my body grow warmer in response. "A summoning spell?"

"I'm sure it's advanced level magic, but how impressive

would I be if I managed it?" One successful language spell and confidence was suddenly seeping from my pores.

Alec scanned the rest of the spell. "I'm no expert, but it seems quite involved."

"I'm summoning a spirit," I said. "It can't be as easy as ordering a pizza for takeout or everyone would be doing it."

"Are you certain it's safe?"

I hesitated. "I don't know. It's magic. I guess there are always risks."

"What if you summon the wrong spirit?" he asked. "What if it's a demon or…?"

I gave him a quick kiss on the lips. "Now you sound like me. Don't worry. I'm not going to summon some hot demon and replace you—unless he shows up with a box of fudge. I'm a sucker for homemade fudge."

"So you think you can simply summon Ivy's spirit and ask her all your questions directly?" Alec asked.

"Why not?"

Concern passed over the vampire's handsome features. "There are very few shortcuts in life, Ember. You know this."

"It doesn't mean I shouldn't try."

"Perhaps I should stay for the summoning, in case something goes awry."

I placed my palm flat against his sculptured cheek. "I appreciate that you want to protect me, but I can handle this."

His fingers curled around my hand and he pressed his lips to it. "I believe in you."

I released the breath I'd been holding. "Good, because I was trying to convince myself. I'm glad you're on board."

"Will you attempt this on your own or ask your cousins for help?"

"I'm going to assemble a team, but not my cousins."

He launched an eyebrow. "Dare I ask?"

I turned back to the grimoire. "Probably best not to."

"I need to send my revisions to the editor and then I have a dinner engagement," Alec said.

"Oh, an engagement, huh? Trying to make me jealous?"

He returned to the sofa to pack up his belongings. "It's with Palmina and Darren at the printing company. We need to discuss *Vox Populi*'s contract. It's up for renewal."

"Okay, that definitely doesn't make me jealous. Have fun."

"I'll speak to you later." He gave one final, lingering kiss before striding out the door.

Thank the gods you two didn't get funky on the sofa. I turned to see Raoul emerge from behind the scratching post. *It was touch and go there earlier.*

"Raoul, how on earth did you manage to hide in plain sight all this time?"

He tapped the black strip of fur across his eyes. *Burglar, remember?*

"You're not a burglar and that black band doesn't make you invisible."

I beg to differ. I've been watching you for two hours. You're surprisingly restrained with each other. What's the problem?

"There's no problem. We're taking things slowly."

That's weird. You two should be spending half your days naked at this point in the relationship period.

"There is no 'should.' We're doing what makes sense for us." I turned back to the grimoire.

He climbed onto the table. *Were you serious about this summoning spell? Because I'm totally into it.*

"You're not a witch," I said.

No, but I'm your familiar. I can help.

"Being annoying is the opposite of helping. Look it up."

I'm serious. Me, you, Marley, and Bonkers, he said. *We can make this happen. Familiars can channel your energy, remember? Besides, it'll be a nice bonding moment for you and the kid.*

He had a point. "I'll consider it."

The door flew open and Marley entered the cottage with Bonkers flying above her shoulder. "Consider what?"

"You just missed Alec," I said.

"I saw him." She kicked off her shoes. "What are you considering? It sounds mysterious and important."

"How's Florian?" I asked. "Did you beat him at cards again?"

She smiled. "He thinks I'm using magic. I keep telling him it's my brain, but he doesn't believe me."

"Well, your brain *is* magical."

Marley came to look over my shoulder. "Ivy's grimoire, huh? I haven't seen you this obsessed with something since Tony's Pizza put cheese-stuffed crust on the menu."

I stopped reading for a moment to enjoy that blissful memory. "Great balls of popcorn. It was amazing."

"Why are you reading about a summoning spell?" Marley asked.

I tapped my fingernails on the book, debating whether to include her. Raoul was right—this could be a nice bonding experience. It could also boost Marley's morale if we get it right. While she wasn't in deep in the doldrums anymore, she still wasn't operating at peak Marley confidence.

"How would you like to help me perform this?"

Her face brightened. "Seriously? You want us to perform a spell from Ivy's grimoire—together?"

"I do." Her excitement was contagious and I felt my own enthusiasm increasing.

She clapped her hands. "Can we do it now?"

"How about after dinner?" I asked. "You don't want to summon on an empty stomach."

Truer words were never spoken, Raoul said, raising a paw. *I'll take a pastrami on rye.*

"I can make dinner if you want to gather what we need

for the spell," Marley said. She started for the kitchen, but then turned back to me. "Or maybe you should do dinner and I'll do spell prep." She seemed torn.

"Are you worried about me screwing up dinner?"

Her gaze shifted to the floor. "Of course not. You've mastered the microwave *and* the toaster now."

Raoul rolled his eyes. *Just order food for delivery and then you can both work on the spell. Problem solved.*

"Gods, I hate it when you make sense," I said. "Why don't we order, Marley?"

She leaned over the table to fist bump Raoul's paw. "Always thinking, Raoul."

About food, he added with a self-satisfied grin.

I ordered sushi from King of the Sea, owned by a friend of Zale's, and Marley and I focused on the requirements of the spell.

"I'll get the chalk from my art supplies," Marley said. She returned a moment later with a chunky piece of white chalk. "I should probably draw the circle."

"Why can't I draw it?"

"You know why," she said vaguely.

"What are you talking about? Are you suggesting that your mother is incapable of drawing a basic circle?"

Marley hesitated. "Don't you remember when you used to help me draw pumpkins for Halloween decorations?"

"But pumpkins aren't completely round," I objected. "They're more like a bumpy oval."

"Be that as it may, I think it's best that we don't risk a bumpy oval for a sophisticated summoning spell. We don't want to accidentally summon the headless horseman."

I frowned. "What does that...Oh, he wore a pumpkin in place of the head, didn't he?"

The doorbell rang and PP3 went charging at the delivery

man. He was going to be disappointed when he smelled the sushi. I paid for the food and Raoul put plates on the table.

"It takes a village," I said.

By the time I set out the food and poured the drinks, Marley had drawn the perfect chalk circle on the floor in front of the door. It was really the only space with enough room to perform the spell. She'd also managed to draw several symbols around the perimeter. They matched the images in the grimoire exactly.

"Do your talents ever end?" I asked, shaking my head in disbelief.

"You said dad could draw," she said. "Maybe this is something I got from him."

I smiled. "I bet it is." Karl wasn't exactly an artist, but he liked to draw his own comic book characters and cartoon strips. Usually he found time for this particular skill in the middle of math class. One of my favorite drawings was one that he'd given me for my birthday. He'd drawn me as Wonder Woman. Of course my boobs had been ten times their normal size and my waist ten times smaller, but how could I begrudge my teenaged boyfriend his fantasy?

"Come and eat," I said. "Then we can focus on the spell."

We scarfed down our sushi. Bonkers was too busy making good use of the scratching post to eat. I made sure to save her a few rolls in case she decided she was hungry later. She was particularly fond of tuna.

"I'll get the candles," Marley said. She barely swallowed the last of her sushi before escaping from the table to get to work. She disappeared into the kitchen to hunt for materials.

I looked at my familiar. "What about you? How are you participating in this group effort?"

He tried to snake one of Bonkers' sushi rolls and I smacked his paw away.

I'm going to sit in the circle and look pretty. What do you expect?

I cleared away the plates. "I should've known."

Marley set up all the candles and I placed my wand on the floor next to the circle. I pointed at Raoul. "Don't even think about going near an open flame once these candles are lit," I warned. "I don't trust you with fire."

And I don't trust you with hair gel, but I can't seem to prevent you from using it.

I brought the grimoire to the circle and sat cross-legged on the floor. "Once I light the candles, we should sit in the circle and hold hands."

Marley whistled for Bonkers, who reluctantly withdrew her claws from the scratching post and joined us. "It might be easier if we hold her wings so we have a little bit more room."

We stretched as far apart as we could, leaving enough room in the circle for Ivy's spirit to appear. I was surprised that Marley didn't seem the least bit anxious. After all, we were inviting a ghost into the cottage. It was the kind of thing that would have made her lose sleep for a month a year ago. My little girl was growing up right before my eyes.

"I need to translate the text back to its original language for the incantation," I said.

"That makes sense," Marley said. "Is it Latin?"

"Not sure. Hold on." I picked up my wand and tapped it on the page, casting the spell. The English faded and was quickly replaced by an unfamiliar language. "I'll read the words the best I can."

I used a simple fire spell to light the candles using the tip of my wand. We joined hands and I performed the incantation slowly and carefully, trying my level best not to mispronounce anything, no small feat given that I had no clue what the language was. The air grew cooler and an Arctic breeze blasted through the cottage, nearly blowing out the candles. Thankfully, the last few words of the spell were in English.

"Rise up," I intoned. "Rise up. We entreat you from the other side. Rise up."

Energy crackled between us, creating sparks of yellow light in the air. Magic rippled through the circle and an image began to form. I could no longer see the symbols that Marley had drawn. They'd been replaced by... a honeycomb? I stared at the floor. Yes, it was definitely a honeycomb. A bee appeared in one of the pockets, followed by another. An entire hive of bees popped into existence. The sound of buzzing grew louder and stronger. To her credit, Marley continued to hold onto Raoul and Bonkers. I worried that her fear of getting stung would cause her to let go. At this point, I couldn't tell whether these were phantom bees or real ones.

The buzzing insects swarmed within the circle above the honeycomb. Eventually a single bee rose above the rest as though overseeing her subjects. The queen. I wasn't sure what I had done wrong to yield this result instead of Ivy's spirit, but there was nothing to do except roll with it. I watched in horror as some bees were drained of life and then summarily kicked out of the honeycomb, their lifeless carcasses lying on the floor outside the circle. Nature at its finest.

Marley gasped when a smaller group of bees danced around the queen. At first I thought it was some sort of a show of respect—until they attacked her. They ripped out her stinger and she dropped to the center of the circle, quickly enveloped by the rest of the hive. Another gust of wind blew through the room, extinguishing the flames all at once.

Marley's voice quivered in the darkness. "Mom?"

By the time I conjured a quick spell to light the tip of my

wand, the circle was empty and no sign of the bees remained. The four of us stared blankly at each other, unsure how to interpret the events.

Well, unless you believe in reincarnation, Raoul said, *I don't think that was your long-lost cousin, Ivy.*

"No, I don't think it was Ivy either," I said. "I must have screwed up one of the words."

One? Try all of them.

"Bees are brutal," Marley whispered. She rested on her knees and stared at the empty circle. She seemed shell-shocked by what she'd witnessed.

"Well, we learned something today, even if it wasn't about Ivy," I said in an effort to look on the bright side.

Marley looked at me. "What's that?"

"Honey is the only thing that's sweet about bees."

"The lone bee dies, but the hive survives," Marley murmured.

"That's wolves," I corrected her.

Marley placed her hand flat where the phantom hive had been. "No, that's everybody."

CHAPTER SIX

PP3's EARS PERKED up and he bolted for the door, barking up a storm.

"Every time I think you're ready for a little doggy cane, you surprise me," I mumbled. I crossed the room to see what the fuss was about and noticed the terrier sniffing a folded piece of paper on the doormat. I picked it up and read the contents—

Dear Ms. Rose,

There is a matter of a great importance being discussed at tonight's Council of Elders meeting that I think might be of interest to you. For the sake of Starry Hollow, I hope you will consider attending.

Anonymously yours,
 Arthur Rutledge

. . .

P.S. - You didn't receive this from me.

P.P.S. - This note will self-destruct in one minute. Misty helped me with the destruction spell, but please don't mention her name either.

The note disintegrated in my hand and I blew away the dust particles. "Commendable job, Missy."

"What was that?" Marley asked. She'd come down from her bedroom where she'd been working on a writing assignment for homework. Although she was disappointed not to be practicing magic, she loved writing so much that she didn't complain—not that Marley ever complained about homework.

"A note inviting me to the Council of Elders meeting tonight," I said.

Her expression brightened. "Why? Are you getting an award?"

I snorted. "For what? Underachiever of the Year?" Despite my aunt's great hope for me, I was proving to be somewhat of a magical disappointment. I had potential—most coven members agreed on that score—but seemed to lack the ability to apply it to the full extent of my abilities.

"Then why?"

"Not sure. The note was vague and a little weird."

"Do you need to ask Florian to get Bell, Book, or Candle from the stable?"

I debated whether I should, but that would lead to questions I couldn't answer. My cousin might also slip to Aunt Hyacinth, who would be in attendance. Obviously, Arthur Rutledge didn't intend for my aunt to know about my invitation or he would have arranged for her to bring me.

"I'll walk," I decided. "I think I know the way."

"Through the woods in the middle of the night?" Marley's voice rose an octave.

"I'll have my wand and my Jersey attitude," I said reassuringly. "It'll be fine."

"What about me?" Marley asked.

"You have a better wand than I do," I said. Of course, we had to remove the negative energy from the family heirloom before it could be used to its full potential and that was proving challenging.

Her blue eyes rounded. "You're going to leave me home alone? On a school night?"

"Of course not." I considered the options. I couldn't send for Mrs. Babcock without word getting back to my aunt before she left. The brownie lived in the main house and would inevitably tell someone where she was going.

"What about Florian?"

"No. I can call Alec." The vampire would either be spending the evening on his book or brooding. Or brooding in the book. He excelled in angst.

Marley clapped her hands. "Yes, please!" She and Alec were devoted members of the mutual admiration society.

As I finished sending a text to the vampire, Raoul appeared in the kitchen doorway.

"Where did you come from?" I asked.

I was in the pantry looking for a snack.

"Alec is coming to hang out while I go to a meeting," I said. "You should probably make yourself scarce."

Are you suggesting he doesn't like me? I'm your familiar. Not liking me is basically the same as not liking you.

"That's not remotely true," I said. "You and I have very different personalities."

Raoul wandered over to the scratching post and began to dig his claws into the carpet.

"What are you doing?" I asked.

After I showed Bonkers how to use it, I realized that it feels kind of good. Thought I'd give it another go.

"No, I need you to go." I hurried upstairs to grab an extra layer for the meeting. There'd be a nip in the air by the time I made my way to the secret location, so I pulled a red hoodie from my closet with *I'm Basic* written across the chest and slipped it over my head. One of Florian's overnight guests had left it behind and refused to return his calls, so he gave it to me.

I stopped by Marley's bedroom where she was showered and in pajamas. "I won't stay up late," she promised. "I have a quiz tomorrow and I don't want to be tired."

"You're so good." I kissed her forehead.

"Since I'm so good, can Alec and I play one game before I go to bed?"

I narrowed my eyes. "Ooh, well played."

Alec was in the living room by the time we came downstairs. He agreed to one round of cards and then Marley dutifully went to bed.

"You're not going to tell me what this clandestine meeting is about?" he asked.

"I can't because I don't know," I said.

"Ride your broomstick," Alec said. "It's safer."

"Landing is tricky in that area because of the trees. I'm better off on two feet." I stood on my tiptoes to kiss him.

"I beg to differ." He gripped my shoulders and deepened the kiss. With his tongue in my mouth, it was hard not to abandon the meeting and just melt against him for the rest of the night. I finally managed to tear myself away.

"I need to go or I'll miss the meeting."

A strange sound shifted my attention to the corner of the room. Raoul stood on one of the platforms of the scratching post, intent on digging his claws into the plush carpet.

"Do you mind?" I said.

The raccoon gave me a guilty look. *I wasn't spying on you. I just really needed to file this nail. It was crooked and driving me nuts.*

Stop being a pervert.

I think I should escort you to the meeting. If any animals give you a hard time, I'll deal with them.

"It's the woods in Starry Hollow," I said. "It's not like we have lions or bears."

No, but we have shifters that can fit that description.

"Fine. You can escort me, but you have to wait outside the cave. No one can know you came with me."

Deal.

We left the cottage and I ran through the woods at a rapid clip—not too fast, though. I didn't want to arrive at the meeting all sweaty with my hair plastered to my forehead. I kept the red hood on to prevent the wind from giving me an earache. As I leaped over a fallen branch, I heard a low growl to my left. I slowed my pace and peered into the darkness.

We've got company, Raoul said, appearing on a branch above my head.

"Who's there?" I called. My fingers tightened around my wand, ready to pull it from my hoodie pocket at a moment's notice.

A large wolf stepped into the moonlight and I recognized Wyatt's disheveled fur. I released my wand and gave a cautious wave. You could never be too sure how he'd behave when he was in his primal form.

"Hey, Wyatt," I said, trying to sound as casual as possible.

Another wolf emerged from the trees, his eyes shining brightly. The wolves began to circle me soundlessly, which almost made me more nervous than the growling. There was something familiar about the second wolf.

"Good evening, boys," I said. "What big teeth you have." I laughed awkwardly.

The second wolf bared his fangs and I jumped slightly.

I'm feeling hostility in the air, Raoul said.

Thank you, Captain Obvious.

I focused on the second wolf. "Granger?" I'd seen him as a wolf before—once when he was very ill and locked in his animal form.

The wolf stopped and seemed to see me for the first time. He sniffed the air close to me and then howled before running between the trees. Wyatt quickly followed. I stood there in silence until the darkness had swallowed them both.

What's up with your ex?

"He's going through a phase," I said.

Of the moon, apparently.

I carried on without another word. I didn't want to risk missing any of the meeting.

"Welcome, Ms. Rose," Arthur said, acting surprised when I finally entered the cave. "What brings you here?"

I nearly said 'you did,' but caught myself. "I understand there's a matter of importance up for debate tonight."

"And who told you that?" Victorine Del Bianco scrutinized me. "Only the elders should be privy to such information."

"I'm not at liberty to reveal my source," I said.

"Welcome, niece," Aunt Hyacinth said coolly. "I didn't realize you planned to intend or I would have escorted you."

"No need for a chaperone." And no need to tell them about the incident in the woods either. "So where are we in this discussion?"

My aunt used her wand to cast a spell and a chair materialized beside her at the round stone table. She motioned for me to sit.

"We are discussing the current issue with Sheriff Nash,"

Missy Brookline said. The fairy's yellow cloak was designed to accommodate her delicate wings.

I stiffened. "What issue?"

"He's been…not himself," Mervin O'Malley said. The leprechaun lowered his gaze, seemingly uncomfortable with the conversation. "He's been acting strangely with residents. I've had reports from my place of business that he's flirting with every female within a wolf-whistle radius."

"He's a bachelor in the prime of his life," Arthur said. "What's the harm?"

"You want to fire him because of excessive flirting?" I added.

"Unfortunately, it's interfering with his ability to perform his duties as sheriff," Oliver Dagwood said. The wizard wore a somber expression and I knew he took no pleasure in saying that.

"Not to mention that some residents no longer feel comfortable with someone like him in charge of our safety and welfare," Mervin said.

"We are of the opinion that he should be replaced," Victorine said.

"Not all of us," Arthur countered. "There hasn't been a vote yet."

Victorine pounded a fist on the table. "Shayna Masters has been murdered and we have no answers. A murderer walks among us and Sheriff Nash is spending his time in bars and prowling the woods like a common wolf. Our standards are higher than that for our sheriff."

"The investigation is still ongoing," I said. "He doesn't spend every waking moment on the case. That's unreasonable. And since when does a murder get solved in a matter of days unless someone confesses?"

"But he isn't working on the case," Amaryllis said gently. "At all."

"How do we know?" I asked. "Are we stalking him?"

Aunt Hyacinth looked at me, her jaw set. "He's been under observation since we were alerted to the situation. We know, for example, that you attempted to reason with him at the Wishing Well but to no avail."

My heart sank. The Council of Elders was better than the FBI. "Sheriff Nash is going through a difficult period, but I promise it won't last. He'll snap out of it and be back to his law-enforcing self in no time."

"We appreciate your belief in him, Ember, but how can you be certain?" Oliver asked. "We can't risk the safety of our residents on a belief. We need to act."

I slotted my fingers together, thinking. "Give him a week to make progress," I said. "If he doesn't work on the case this week, then feel free to fire him."

"That's not good enough," Victorine snarled. "The victim had marks on her neck. Do you know what happens when someone dies in this town with marks on their neck?"

"But the marks are evidence of strangulation," I said. "Not fangs."

Victorine's expression hardened. "Do you think those details matter? Rumors beget rumors and then it's chaos. We cannot risk it."

"I hate to say it, but I agree with Victorine," Mervin said.

"Okay, then how about this?" I proposed. "If Shayna's murder isn't solved in a week, then go ahead and replace him." A lump formed in my throat at the thought of someone else pinning that star on their chest.

"Solved in a week?" Arthur echoed. He sounded as nervous as I felt.

"That's right," I said. "If Shayna's killer is caught within the week, then Sheriff Nash keeps his job."

"Fine, but we'll still need to address his behavior," Victorine said. "The town will be slapped with a harassment suit if it keeps up. He's becoming a liability that we can't afford."

"Deal," I said.

"Are we all in agreement?" my aunt asked, addressing the rest of the elders.

"Aye," they said unison.

"You'll deliver our message, Ember?" Mervin asked.

"Don't worry. I'll tell him what he needs to know," I said vaguely. I wasn't sure exactly what that would entail because I didn't want to risk pushing him away by being the bearer of bad news. All I knew right now was that Granger needed my help and I was determined to give it to him—whether he wanted it or not.

CHAPTER SEVEN

I STOOD on the doorstep of Haverford House, feeling a twinge of guilt that I came without Marley. She and Artemis adored each other, but the conversations I needed to have with the elderly witch were better kept between us. Although Marley and I were close, that didn't mean it was appropriate for her to know everything going on in my life. Boundaries were a necessity, for her sake as well as mine.

"I'm so pleased to see you," Artemis said. She wore a pale, peach-colored dress trimmed in lace, and her white hair was loose and adorned with a matching ribbon. She tended to look a century behind and today was no exception.

"I hope you don't mind the unexpected visit."

"Of course not, and on a weekday no less. Do come in." She shuffled into the parlor and I followed. "Jefferson, tea for two, please."

"Hi, Jefferson," I called to her ghostly manservant.

We settled around the coffee table and Clementine came running to greet me. I could tell by the stiff swish of her tail that she was annoyed to find Marley absent.

"Now, now," Artemis said. "Marley is at school. I imagine Ember must want to indulge in an adult conversation today."

"Well, I try to avoid those as much as possible," I joked.

Artemis wore a vague smile, the wrinkles around her mouth giving her face a puckered look. "Tell me how she's getting on at the academy. Have they offered early graduation yet?"

"Ha, not quite," I said. "She's doing well, though. Thanks for asking."

"Please send her my regards."

"You can tell her yourself next time I bring her to see you," I said. "Today is more of a necessary visit than a social call."

"I assumed as much. How can I help, dear?"

A tray with a teapot and two cups floated into the room and came to rest on a sideboard. I watched as Jefferson poured the tea and delivered the two cups on saucers to the coffee table.

"Thanks, Jefferson," I said. I felt a cool rush of air as the ghost vacated the parlor. Even in ghost form, he was the consummate professional.

"What's on your mind, Ember?"

"I guess I'll start with your prophecy about my aunt's romantic life."

Her wrinkled brow lifted. "My prophecy?"

"Whatever you want to call it," I said. "Remember, she came here and you predicted three suitors and one was a wolf in sheep's clothing or something." Or maybe I just had wolf on the brain.

"And what's the question, dear?"

"There's this wizard, Craig," I said. "He just seems too good to be true and Aunt Hyacinth is head over heels, for her." I shook my head. "I'm starting to think I don't trust him."

Artemis folded her hands primly in her lap. "Well, you've always had good instincts, dear. I'm certainly not going to sit here and advise you to ignore them."

"Good, because I can't," I said. "He has to be the one you said to watch out for. He's just so smooth and refined."

"Sounds like someone else you know," Artemis said. She blew off the steam and sipped of her tea.

"Who do I know like that?" I asked. I swallowed a mouthful of tea and took another sip.

"Mr. Hale, of course," the elderly witch said. "The vampire you happen to be head over heels in love with."

I nearly spat my tea all over my lap. "You think Craig and Alec are similar? No way."

"Maybe it's your inner voice projecting your fears about Alec onto this other man."

"I don't have any fears about Alec," I said. "I trust him. Besides, I never said I was in love with him."

Artemis cackled softly. "Ember, please. I recognize the signs. I've been there myself once or twice. There's no shame in it."

"I'm not ashamed," I said. "Alec is amazing. I'd be lucky to…We're talking about Craig right now. Let's stick to that."

"As you wish." She stroked Clementine, now curled up beside her.

"What do I do?" I asked.

"What do you want to do?"

"I want to make sure Craig isn't taking advantage of my aunt," I said.

"And what if he is? She's a grown woman. A very powerful witch. You don't think she can handle herself?"

"I don't think she's ever been swept off her feet before, not like this." I paused. "I mean Zale literally swept her off her feet when he carried her out of the sea, but Craig is something else. The way she looks at him…"

"What of it?"

I set down my cup and saucer. "It's the way I catch myself looking at Alec sometimes, like he's a gift to the world and I get to keep him on behalf of a grateful earth."

She smiled. "That's a very special feeling. You should cherish it."

"But if Craig is…I don't know…evil or something."

"I don't think I predicted an evil predator. I believe there were three suitors—" She strained to listen to something I couldn't hear. "Yes, Jefferson, I believe you're correct." She shifted back to me. "A gentleman who comes from humble beginnings, but has set himself apart, whether through business or magic or some other means. Someone seductive and charming. He may seem like what she wants, but ultimately he will leave her feeling alone, and then someone who will take her by surprise and offer her a ride worth taking. Bumpy and uncomfortable at times, but exhilarating."

"Okay, so Craig is the snake. Seductive and charming but will leave her feeling alone."

"That doesn't necessarily make him evil or someone to avoid," Artemis said. "A failed relationship can still bestow lessons she must learn in order to progress in her next relationship."

"So you think Craig isn't out to hurt my aunt or steal all her money?"

"I have no idea," Artemis said. "I don't know the wizard. Your aunt has never been one to suffer from poor judgment, though."

"That's because she's never been in crazy love. Anyone who's ever been in crazy love knows that your judgment suffers."

Artemis eyed me closely. "What makes you certain that your aunt is so smitten?"

"For starters, she remembered his favorite drink from holiday dinners."

The elderly witch chuckled. "A consummate hostess makes a point of remembering such seemingly minor details."

"Stop sounding so practical and wise."

"Isn't that why you seek my counsel?" She patted my hand. "You need to let this play out as it should, Ember. I don't advise interfering in your aunt's relationships. She won't thank you for it, no matter how right you are. It isn't her way."

"No, you're right. She'll resent me." When Karl and I were getting serious, I remembered asking my father why he didn't break us up. We were so young and I knew he'd object. He said he'd rather support me and be there when things fell apart than have me push him away and not be there when I needed him. Of course, my dad didn't live long enough to see the end of our story. First my dad. Then Karl. Inwardly, I shuddered. Maybe Artemis was right. Maybe I did have fears about Alec, but not the kind she insinuated. More like fear that I'll lose him the way I'd lost the two other men I…

"Ember, dear?"

I snapped to attention. "Yes?"

"What's your other issue? You suggested a second one."

"Right." I cleared my throat. "Something strange is going on with the sheriff."

"How so?"

"He's been acting…more wolf than man," I said. "More like Wyatt, in fact, and others have noticed. There's a murder investigation underway and Sheriff Nash seems more interested in chasing tail than chasing suspects." To quote Deputy Bolan.

"How unfortunate," Artemis said. "I can see why that's a problem, but how can I help?"

"Can we do one of your insightful card games to see if we can figure out what's causing it?" I asked. "I want to help him, but I don't know how."

"Hmm. You seem to be very invested in helping those who may not want it."

"Can you blame me? What if the sheriff is acting out because of me?"

Artemis patted my hand. "Granger Nash is an adult. If he's misbehaving, I imagine it's a passing phase that he needs to work through to get to the other side of his feelings."

"That's what I keep saying, but I don't know. You don't think it's possible someone put a spell on him to make him act this way?"

"For what purpose?" she asked.

I'd been struggling to answer that one already. "I don't know. An old enemy?"

"An old enemy wants him to get lucky with the ladies?" Artemis clucked her tongue. "Ember, your feelings are clouding your judgment. This isn't just your guilt talking, you know."

"It is," I insisted.

She gave my hand one more squeeze and let go. "It's perfectly acceptable to care about him, even though you chose someone else. We don't turn our emotions off and on like the faucet."

"Do you even turn your own faucet on? Because I'm pretty sure Jefferson does it."

She smiled. "Jefferson most certainly turns my faucet off and on."

Inwardly, I cringed. For a fleeting moment, I'd forgotten about their unusual relationship. I'd like to forget again. There had to be a potion for that.

"I don't want the sheriff to lose his job," I said. "How do I fix him?"

"He isn't a toy, Ember, nor is he yours to fix."

"I promised that the murder would be solved within a week so that he could keep his job," I admitted. Of course, I never promised that Granger would be the one solving it.

Artemis took a long sip of her tea. "Well then, a week isn't long at all, is it? If you're set on helping him, I suppose you ought to get to work."

Alec breezed into the office of *Vox Populi* and dropped by my desk for a kiss. "All alone in this big office?"

"Bentley's still sailing one of the seven seas and Tanya has an appointment."

He peered at my screen. "You seem very intent on something."

"I'm typing notes on everything I know about Shayna Masters."

"For an article?"

I had to tell him the truth. Mostly because I didn't want to keep secrets from my boyfriend. Also, because I was going to be busy with this case while Bentley was on his honeymoon. As my boss, Alec needed to know what I was up to.

"I have to help Deputy Bolan solve Shayna's murder, only he doesn't know it yet."

"Which one?"

I swallowed hard. "Both."

Alec regarded me. "Is the sheriff incapacitated?"

"Sort of." I explained what was happening and shared the council's ultimatum. "But you can't breathe a word. I don't want to fuel the gossip flames."

Alec perched on the edge of my desk. "It seems to me that Nash is simply cycling through the stages of grief."

"Nobody died, Alec."

"No, but his hope did," the vampire replied. "He's grieving the loss of your relationship, of what could have been."

That actually made more sense than revenge by an old enemy. "So, if you're right, what happens next?"

"He should eventually work through each stage until he reaches acceptance."

"Out of curiosity, which stage is douche canoe in? Because that's where he's stuck right now and it's threatening his career."

His mouth twitched. "Hmm. I'm not familiar with that particular phase."

"Maybe because it isn't the stages of grief." I picked up a pen for the sole purpose of chucking it across the office. I was so frustrated.

"I have no need to be right, Ember. I'm only trying to help."

"How about by solving this case with us so Granger can keep his job. If he loses his badge, it will be all my fault."

He frowned. "How is his undesirable behavior attributable to you?"

"You said yourself he's cycling through grief because of me. That makes anything that happens as a result my fault."

Alec released a gentle sigh. "Has anyone ever told you that you're too hard on yourself?"

"Mr. Lucky Charms and I are going to band together to help Granger crack this case. I think you'd be an asset, too, but not if you're going to get all bumpy-faced about it."

He suppressed a smile. "Bumpy-faced?"

"You know, that broody vampire face you make. Don't you ever look in the mirror...Oh, forget it."

He leaned down to kiss my cheek. "If it means that much to you, I pledge my assistance."

My spirits soared. "Really?"

"Of course. It also gives us an inside scoop for the article you're going to write about the murder."

I grimaced. "Naturally."

"Bentley is away, so it's all hands on deck, I'm afraid. I'm happy to help Nash, but the paper is still a priority for me."

"Two birds, one Ember. I get it. Thank you for offering to help. It means a lot to me."

"Nash and I don't exactly have the best history, but I'm willing to set that aside for you."

"Oh, yeah. And why is that?" I asked, a teasing note in my voice.

"Because you're my best employee." He gave me another quick kiss before returning to a standing position. "I have an appointment with the tailor, but I'll see you at dinner, yes?"

"Not tonight. I have that girls' night with Linnea and Aster, remember?"

"Ah, yes. The Rose witches all in one place with alcohol. I shall issue the alert."

I chucked an eraser at his head and he caught it the way Mr. Miyagi snatched a fly out of the air with chopsticks in *Karate Kid*. Sweet baby Elvis, that vampire was the sexiest thing on two legs I'd ever seen.

As Alec opened the door to exit, Deputy Bolan walked straight under his extended arm.

"Thanks, Hale," the leprechaun said.

Alec raised his brow at me and slipped out the door.

Deputy Bolan sauntered over to my desk with a cup of coffee in his tiny green hand. "You beckoned, Rose?"

I zeroed in on his cup. "You went to the Caffeinated Cauldron and didn't bring me one? That's just poor manners."

"This from the witch that uses the tip of her wand as a toothpick."

"Hey, that was one time in a spinach emergency!" I inhaled the aroma. "What kind did you get?"

"Lava latte."

I wrinkled my nose. "Okay, I feel better. I don't like that one much anyway."

He scanned the room. "Why are you alone? Did you finally manage to alienate everyone you work with?"

"Bentley is still on his honeymoon and Tanya has an appointment."

"Okay, what's this clandestine meeting about?"

I told him about my deal with the Council of Elders.

"A week," he repeated. He drank half his latte in one gulp. "I guess I can do it if I work around the clock."

"I'm going to help and Alec said he will, too," I said. "I've been working on a list of facts about Shayna."

"No way, Rose. I can do this without you. In fact, I'd prefer to do this without you."

"You have to make it look like Granger is responsible, though. If the council figures out that it's you, that'll just convince them to give you the job."

"He's not comatose," the deputy shot back. "He's just… ineffective right now. I can involve him enough to make him look good. He was with me when I interviewed the berserker, in fact."

"The one in the port-a-potty next to hers?"

The deputy nodded. "Dead end. He heard a commotion but thought a couple was getting busy in the stall. Didn't see who." He paused. "The sheriff seemed to enjoy probing for details."

Ugh.

"What about cause of death?" I asked. "Definitely strangulation?"

"Technically the cause of death is the brooch that choked her."

I balked. "Brooch? You mean that pretty pin in the shape of a flower?"

"That's the one. You saw it?"

"Yes, she wore it at the wedding. I told her I liked it." My stomach turned. "Some monster shoved that brooch down her throat and killed her with it?"

"Not a great way to go, is it?"

I tried to block the images that were flashing in my mind. "She told me it was from her shop. Have you spoken to anyone there?"

"Not yet. I was heading there next, in fact. According to Shayna's lawyer, her niece has inherited the business."

I shot him an aggrieved look. "You already went to the lawyer without me?"

"We can't spend all our time together, Rose. Paranormals will talk."

"You'll have to fill me in on what I missed so I can update my notes. Why'd you come here first? I told you I'd be here for a couple of hours."

The leprechaun shrugged. "You were on the way and sounded needy."

I glared at him. "Your boss is the one in need, Deputy, and I'm willing to help. Don't look a gift horse in the mouth."

The leprechaun relented. "You do seem to be the gift that keeps on giving."

"Like reusable shopping bags?"

"I was thinking more like diarrhea. Come on, Rose."

The interior of Be-switched reminded me more of a Pottery Barn than a resale shop. Every item looked brand-new, from the furniture on the right-hand side of the store to the shelves of decorative objects in the middle. Only the section on the left was clearly used because the items were all identified as antiques. There were ceramic bowls, wooden boxes, and even a case filled with different styles of jewelry.

"Can I help you...?" A young troll stopped short when she noticed Deputy Bolan's badge. "Are you here about Aunt Shayna?"

"That's right. I'm Deputy Bolan and this is my associate, Ms. Ember Rose."

"I'm Shayna's niece, Lois. I work here part-time." She paused. "Well, I guess I'm full-time now until her estate gets sorted."

"I understand from her lawyer that she left this place to you," the deputy said. "Did you know that?"

"She mentioned it to me once or twice, but I never gave it much thought until she died. My aunt was the kind of paranormal that you picture living forever, you know? She was larger than life and not just because she was a troll."

"This place is a big responsibility," I said. "At least you've been working here part-time and know the ropes."

"I'll be honest. I regret that we didn't have a conversation about it. I'm not sure that I really want the shop. I'd been thinking about going back to school, but now I feel obligated to keep this place going in her memory. Be-switched was her life's work."

"Would you consider selling it?" I asked.

Lois shook her head. "I think I would feel too guilty. My boyfriend says I'm being ridiculous and I should just do what's best for me." She gnawed on a fingernail. "I need to give it some time. I feel like any decision I make right now will be too emotional."

Well, Lois may have been young, but she seemed to have a good head on her shoulders.

"I guess you must've been working while she attended the wedding with Franco," I said.

Lois nodded. "She liked to stay open longer hours on weekends because of paranormals being off work and weekend tourists. I didn't leave here on until around nine that night."

"Are you aware of any issues that your aunt may have had with customers—or anyone at all really?" I asked.

Lois snorted. "When you have a personality like Aunt Shayna did, you tended to have issues with others. Don't get me wrong, I loved her dearly, but I can't sit here and pretend that she was universally liked."

"Any recent incidents that you can think of?" Deputy Bolan asked.

"Well there was the whole shooting at the neighbor thing."

I blinked. "Say what?"

"I don't mean that she shot anyone for real," Lois said. "She'd gotten a set of antique pistols and was apparently testing to see whether they were still usable."

Deputy Bolan scratched his ear. "I think I remember this. It was about two weeks ago, right? The sheriff mentioned it in passing."

Lois gestured to the neighboring shop. "She scared the life out of that poor wizard in Quicksilver."

"Was anybody hurt?" I asked.

"No, and Aunt Shayna was thrilled that the pistols worked. Plenty of bullets, too."

"Any chance we can see a recent customer list?" Deputy Bolan asked.

"Do you want to see customers who purchased items or customers who brought in items for resale?" Lois moved behind the counter and logged in on the computer.

"Both," the deputy said. "I'll start with customers she interacted with this month."

"That's easy," Lois said, tapping on the keys. "Be-switched isn't like a regular retailer. Our customer base is more fixed."

"What about tourists?" I asked. "Isn't that why you said you work keep the shop open longer on weekends?"

"Those are mostly browsers," Lois said. "Aunt Shayna was always afraid of missing an opportunity. It was almost a compulsion with her. She was the same in her personal life. She was engaged three times before she met Franco, did you know that?"

Deputy Bolan and I exchanged glances. "No, I didn't know that," I said.

"She never married any of them," Lois said. "I think she only agreed to the engagement because she didn't want to turn down the chance to get married."

"Did she have something against marriage or was she never that serious about them in the first place?" I asked.

The printer came to life and Lois went to retrieve the customer list for Deputy Bolan. "She always said marriage wasn't a priority. She liked things done her own way and wasn't big on compromise. I get the sense that the minute she had to compromise on something important to her, she bailed."

"Any sense that she was serious about Franco?" I asked.

"She only made one comment that stood out to me," Lois said. "And that was that she was surprised that he hadn't proposed yet. I couldn't tell you whether she was disappointed or just mildly interested that he hadn't."

"Any recent interactions with a former fiancé that you know of?" Deputy Bolan asked.

"The only one I'm aware of is Todd Andersen. He was fiancé number two. She ran into him a couple weeks ago at Elixir. I don't know what happened, but she seemed unsettled by it."

"Thanks for the list," the deputy said. "Anything else noteworthy that you can think of?"

"There is one thing," Lois said. "I've been going through

inventory, just in case I decide to sell and I noticed that an item is missing from the jewelry case."

"Do you know what it is?" I asked.

"A brooch in the shape of a flower. One of her regular customers brought it in."

"Did it have different colored gemstones?" I asked.

Her brow lifted. "How did you know?"

"We have the brooch," Deputy Bolan said. "Your aunt was wearing it at the wedding. I'm afraid we need to keep it as evidence."

"Just because she was wearing it? Do you need to keep all her personal effects?"

I shifted uncomfortably. Neither one of us wanted to explain to Lois why we couldn't return the brooch.

"I'm afraid that the brooch is off the market," Deputy Bolan said, and left it at that.

"Aunt Shayna would be disappointed," Lois said. "Some famous socialite used to own it. She liked that sort of thing." Her gaze swept the shop. "She liked all these things." Her expression grew pained. "Now what do I do?"

I gave her arm a comforting squeeze. "The only thing you can do now, Lois," I said. "You grieve."

CHAPTER EIGHT

"Great Goddess of the Moon, what is that ungodly thing?" Hazel pointed to the scratching post in my living room, her face frozen in horror.

"One of Raoul's recent treasures."

"Can we cloak it during the lesson? It's distracting."

"So is your face, but I still muddle through each week."

Hazel glowered at me. "Yes, I think muddle is the optimum word there."

"Can we skip runes today?" I asked.

The Mistress of Runecraft looked ready to burst several blood vessels. "Why would I agree to such a thing?"

"Because you're a generous soul with…" I trailed off. "Nah, forget it. How about because I want to?"

"If you're not careful, Marley is going to surpass you in runes when she's only just begun her studies."

"Marley surpassed me when she learned object permanence."

The witch sat across from me and threaded her fingers together. "What is it that you'd like to do instead, bearing in mind that I'm not watching a TED Talk on getting in touch with your inner Springsteen, whatever that means."

"Stop checking out my browser history," I said. "It's rude."

She pursed her cherry red lips. "It's none of my business, but some of those more intimate questions you ask Mr. Google could be answered by the vampire himself. He knows his own body best, after all."

I pointed a finger at her. "You're right. None of your business."

"What is it that you want to learn, Ember? At this point, I'm willing to entertain other options, as long as you're learning *something*."

"I want to learn more about herbs."

"That's an entirely...reasonable request and not at all what I expected." Hazel contemplated me. "Why not ask Calla?"

"Oh, I can," I said. "It's just that my schedule is already so crammed. The thought of adding another subject into my regular rotation is too overwhelming. I'd rather ditch runes for something useful."

"I'll pretend you didn't say that." Hazel stretched her arms. "I guess I could help you. Are you trying to learn about any herbs in particular?"

"I'd like to help Marley with her garden," I said. "I kill everything and this garden is really important to her, so I don't want to screw it up."

"I see. That's actually very sweet of you." She hesitated. "I thought you were going to tell me that you want to concoct a mixture that makes your aunt more agreeable or something like that." She cleared her throat. "Which I *never* would have helped with, so don't even consider asking."

"Aunt Hyacinth isn't much of an issue right now, not with Craig hovering around her like some kind of hunky gnat."

Hazel smiled to herself. "She does seem smitten. It's a rare occasion when your aunt whistles and it isn't to summon someone for a reprimand."

"I'm not sure I like him," I blurted.

Hazel recoiled. "Why ever not? He seems like a perfect gentleman. A wizard from a good family. Money. Attractive."

"Exactly. It's not normal."

"You're not normal," Hazel shot back. She coiled a strand of red hair around her finger, indulging in inappropriate thoughts about Craig, no doubt.

"Any guy that wonderful is hiding a dark secret or he's playing a role because he wants something."

She eyed me closely. "Is this because you're from New Jersey?"

"No, nobody hides anything in New Jersey," I said, shaking my head. "We lay it all out there for everyone to see."

"Do you think Craig is using your aunt for his own personal gain?"

"Maybe."

Hazel heaved a sigh. "Ember, don't you think it's possible that your aunt is just a vivacious woman whom he finds attractive?"

I considered the question for a moment. "No."

Hazel threw her head back and laughed. "Let's keep that one between us."

"Not because I don't think those things about her," I clarified. "I just don't trust Craig. He came out of nowhere. Linden shows up after a long time away with her impossibly perfect cousin in tow." I shrugged. "Something feels off about him."

Hazel appeared thoughtful. "Why don't we combine your request for an herbology lesson with your concerns about Craig?"

"I like where this seems to be going."

Hazel pushed back her chair and stood. "Field trip."

"To where? It's been a busy day and I'm a little tired."

"Relax, lazy bones. To the herb garden out front. Bring a bowl."

"Oh, I can do that." I left the table to retrieve a bowl and followed her.

She stood with her feet shoulder-width apart and her hands on her hips, examining the herb garden. "Your daughter certainly has a knack."

"That's why I keep my distance," I said. "Whatever the opposite of knack is, that's what I have."

"Right, so I see wormwood and elderberries," Hazel said. "We can use those. You'll want some licorice root, too."

I contemplated the tidy garden. "Do I dig them up or what?"

"You can use a spell. Might be safer than letting you loose with gardening tools. I'll hold the bowl so you can cast."

I handed her the bowl, then brandished my wand and aimed it at the wormwood. "How will this mixture help me with Craig?"

"We can cast a spell with it. Just a pinch of this in his drink and he'll speak nothing but the truth for at least an hour."

That sounded promising.

Wormwood separated from the rest of the plant and drifted into the bowl. I shifted my focus to the elderberries and aimed my wand.

"These can be tricky because of the berries," Hazel warned.

The words were scarcely out of her mouth when the elderberries exploded, bits flying in all directions. Even worse, the roots tore from the ground and scattered as well.

"Uh oh," I said. There'd be no hiding this mess from Marley unless I acted quickly.

Hazel bit her lip. "Well, that wasn't what we intended, is it?"

"Marley has music lessons, so I should have time to fix it before she gets home."

Hazel placed the bowl on the ground and dusted herself off. "I'll leave you to it then."

My head swiveled toward her. "What? You're leaving?"

"I don't want to get caught in a mother-daughter squabble. Brings up too many uncomfortable memories."

"You had a mother? And here I thought you were raised by the circus."

Hazel narrowed her eyes at me. "Next lesson we do runes."

"Next week?"

"No, we'll be tacking another lesson on this week. There's no mess when we're dealing with symbols."

"That's not what you usually say about my handwriting."

Hazel took another look at the mess before turning to leave.

"What about the spell?" I called.

"Craig can wait," she replied. "It's not as though he's going anywhere."

No, I thought glumly. *He certainly wasn't.*

"Mom, what are you doing to my garden?"

I froze on my knees where I'd been frantically trying to salvage the elderberries. Slowly, I turned to see Marley at the edge of the yard. "You're home early, sweetheart."

"My music lesson was cancelled, so Bonkers and I walked home." She marched over to gauge the situation. "Why is there a section missing?"

"Well, it's a funny story…"

"Is it?"

My gaze dropped. "No, not really. I was trying to experiment with elderberries and I accidentally destroyed the batch."

"How do you accidentally destroy elderberries?" she demanded. "And why were you experimenting at all?"

"Hazel offered to help me with herbology so that I could be a better caretaker of your garden," I said. A partial truth. "I know how important it is to you and you're obviously a natural. I just want to be more of a help than a hindrance."

Marley's expression softened. "You're trying to learn herbology for me?"

"Of course. You know I'd do anything for you."

She rushed forward and threw her arms around my neck. "You're the best mom in the whole multiverse."

I planted a kiss on her cheek. "Are you watching Marvel movies again?"

"No, I'm reading a book at school by a wizard called Thalan who believed in a multiverse. I'm pretty sure that's where humans got the idea."

I smiled. "Look at you, talking about humans as though you're not one."

"Only half, remember?" She pulled out her wand. "Here, let me help you dig that hole. We'll make it a little deeper this time. I think I went too shallow with the last batch anyway. Maybe that's why the roots came up so easily."

I moved back to let her work. "Don't grip it too tightly. Remember what your teacher said." I didn't recall exactly, but it was something akin to Marley maintaining a death grip on her wand and needing to loosen up. A lesson for life, really.

"We should do the shovel instead of the spade because we want to go deeper this time," Marley said.

"You're the garden boss."

She aimed her wand at the shovel and said, "*Excavo*."

The tool lifted into the air and moved to strike the earth.

The moment it made contact with the ground, it bounced off and landed on its side.

"That's okay, Marley. Try again."

She squared her shoulders and exhaled before raising her wand at the shovel. *"Excavo."*

The spell resulted in the same result. "Here," I said. "Let me try." Part of me hoped to fail so that Marley didn't suffer another blow to her confidence. We'd already endured that not too long ago and she was finally getting back on track.

I focused my will and aimed my wand. *"Excavo."* The shovel bounced off again and landed in the garden with a thud.

"This didn't happen when you planted the herbs the first time," I said.

"No, but I didn't try to go as deep. Maybe there's more rock under the top layer than I realized."

"I don't think that's due to rocks," I said. "It seems more like some kind of protective barrier."

Or a shallow grave, Raoul interjected. *Maybe they moved the headstone but they didn't move the body.*

I whipped around. "Sneaking up on us and throwing in a nightmare scenario?" I said. "Thanks for that." One viewing of *Poltergeist* as a child was enough for me.

"Should we try the old-fashioned way?" Marley asked. She reached down and picked up the shovel.

"Good idea. Maybe the barrier is only for magic rather than plain digging." I grabbed the spade and we started to dig.

Two pizzas says it's a casket, Raoul said.

So if it's not a casket, you owe me two pizzas? I asked.

No. Either way, you owe me two pizzas.

I rolled my eyes and kept digging. The tip of my spade hit something hard. "Marley, there's definitely something here and I don't think it's a rock."

Raoul peered over my shoulder excitedly. *Come on, lucky corpse.*

I heaved away more dirt until I could reach the object. "I think it's a book." The brown cover was worn and faded. I used the spade as leverage to pry the book from its hiding place. Dirt flew in all directions and I coughed.

"Who would bury a book?" Marley asked. "That's so disrespectful."

"Yes," I said with the hint of a smile. "Much worse than dog-earing a page."

"Only monsters do that," Marley shot back.

I wiped away the remaining granules of dirt and set the book on the ground in front of us. "It looks like there used to be words on the cover, but they're too faded to read."

"Maybe we shouldn't open it," Marley said. I heard the anxiety creeping into her voice.

"Why not?" I asked. "Are you afraid something's going to jump out? It's a book, not a box." I turned to give Raoul a pointed look. "Hear that? Not a box."

"What if the book was buried there so that no one could open it?" Marley asked. "What if there's a demon trapped inside or something and we set it free?"

I stared at her. "I told you that you weren't ready to watch Buffy."

Marley exchanged guilty looks with Raoul. "I may have mentioned it to Florian and he liked the idea of a cheerleader turned vampire slayer."

"I'll bet," I said. I'd have to give Florian a tongue-lashing later. Right now I had a mystery book to deal with. "Why don't you go inside the cottage and lock the door?"

Marley balked. "And leave you out here with the book? Do you have a death wish?"

Sometimes I think she does, Raoul said.

"Listen, you watch from the window," I said. "If something goes south, you can call Aunt Hyacinth or Alec." I offered an encouraging smile. "Honestly, sweetheart. I think it'll be fine. It just looks like an old book that somebody wanted to keep safe."

Marley's gaze darted to the book and back to me. "Okay. I do want to know what's in there. Maybe there'll be cool recipes. Or a diary."

Or preserved food, Raoul added.

I narrowed my eyes at the raccoon. "You go with Marley."

Why can't Bonkers do it? She's the familiar.

Because Bonkers is adorable. I need you.

Raoul kicked a pebble before turning toward the cottage. Marley fell into step beside him. I waited until they were safely installed in the cottage before placing my hands on the book. I wasn't sure whether it was my imagination, but I definitely felt energy emanating from the book. I couldn't tell much beyond that.

I sat for a moment with the book in my lap. The handwriting on the cover was long and full of loops, but there was no mistaking the words 'Book of Shadows' and 'Ivy Rose.'

Sweet mother of baby Elvis's pearl!

"I think the summoning spell might have worked after all," I whispered. I hugged the book and ran into the house with it to show the others. "You're never going to believe this."

You found pizza crust that didn't get moldy? Old news. Raoul swatted his paw.

"No." I slapped the book onto the table. "This is Ivy's Book of Shadows. I don't think it's a coincidence."

Marley bounced over to investigate. "You think the summoning spell directed you to find it?"

"I think there's a connection. Maybe Ivy's spirit couldn't speak to us directly, but her Book of Shadows might have something to say instead." I tried to open to the first page, but the cover refused to budge.

"What's wrong?" Marley asked.

"It's warded shut," I said.

Marley tried to pry it open, too, but without success. "I guess it makes sense. If it's personal, she must've warded the way I used to put a lock on my diary."

"You never used a lock," I said. "Not that I would know," I added quickly.

Marley ran a hand across the cover. "I can't believe it. Her Book of Shadows right in my herb garden."

"Let's keep this between us for now," I said. "I'd like to be able to open it before Aunt Hyacinth demands a look at it." Depending on what was inside, maybe we'd never get it back.

"How will you open it?" Marley asked. "She was one of the most powerful witches in our family history. It will take a lot of skill to break one of her spells."

Marley was right. I hadn't even managed to clean the negative energy from her wand yet and Ivy Rose continued to grow more complex by the day. Clearly, Ivy—or someone else—had intended to keep her secrets literally buried. Although I wasn't the powerful witch that Ivy had been, I had another skill in my wheelhouse that they couldn't have anticipated—stubbornness.

After all these years, Ivy Rose's magic was about to meet its match.

CHAPTER NINE

"So what exactly do we do on a girls' night?" Aster asked. We sat in the formal living room of Palmetto House, the inn owned by my cousin Linnea.

"You've never done a girls' night?" I asked. Not that I was one to talk. I could count the number of friends I had in Maple Shade, New Jersey on one hand.

Aster sat on the sofa with her ankles crossed and her hands clasped neatly in her lap. "I suppose there are women at all of the galas and cocktail parties that I attend with Sterling."

I shook my head adamantly. "No, no. That is *not* a girls' night out. The fact that there are women present does not make it one."

Aster gave us a helpless look. "So what are we meant to do? Shall I change into my pajamas?"

"Yes, and right after that we'll braid each other's hair," I said.

"My hair is very fine," Aster said, running a hand through the white-blond tendrils.

I chucked one of the decorative pillows at her head.

"We're not actually doing that. That's like the guy fantasy of what we do."

Aster sighed with relief. "Thank the gods. The thought of either one of you touching my hair was enough to send me for mother's smelling salts."

"How about a drink?" Linnea asked. "I can whip up margaritas."

"What's a margarita?" Aster asked.

"Oh, Ember introduced me to them a few weeks ago," Linnea said. "The mixture of salty and sweet is much more appealing than I would have guessed."

Aster seemed hesitant. "I don't know. I have to leave first thing in the morning to relieve Sterling."

"Hey, I'm impressed that he's stepping up tonight. Major props him."

Aster relaxed slightly. "Yes, I was quite pleased that he agreed to it. He even canceled a meeting in order to be home with the boys. When I mentioned it to Sterling's mother, she said how wonderful it was that he was babysitting so that I could go out and socialize."

Linnea sucked in a breath. "No, she didn't."

"Isn't that absurd?" Aster asked. "Sterling is their father. He doesn't get paid an hourly wage in order to care for his own sons."

"It's generational," Linnea said. "Although, to be fair, Wyatt's mother would never say such a thing. She was the best reason to marry into the Nash family."

"Speaking of the devil," I said, "where did he take Bryn and Hudson tonight?"

"No idea," Linnea said. Aster and I followed her into the kitchen while she set to work making the margaritas. "The unrealistic part of me hopes that they're sitting at a table playing a wholesome game of dominoes tonight, but I know better."

"You think they're playing something that they shouldn't?" I could see Hudson possibly indulging, but Bryn was far too sensible.

"No, I'm afraid that Wyatt is leaving them on their devices while he does whatever he pleases," Linnea said. "You know, the usual. As much as I want them to spend quality time with their father, it never seems to actually result in quality."

"Well, I left Sterling a list of instructions and a timetable," Aster said. "He's meant to check off each item as he completes it."

"Are you testing him?" I asked. "Like you said, he's their father. Maybe you should leave the evening up to him."

Aster laughed. "Sterling wouldn't know what to do with the boys."

"Why not?" I asked. "He was one himself once upon a time. Do you think he's forgotten what it was like?"

Aster tapped her perfectly manicured nails on the counter. "I suppose you have a point. Even so, I think I'll just make a quick call to check on them." She reached for her phone, but Linnea grabbed her by the wrist to stop her.

"Don't even think about it," Linnea said. "You have to show him that you trust him. You don't want to undermine his confidence by constantly checking on him."

Aster slipped her phone back into her pocket. "That makes sense. All right, I'll do my best to focus on girls' night and leave Sterling to boys' night."

"Need any help with those margaritas?" I asked.

Linnea twirled her wand in the air. "I have all the help I need right here, thanks."

Half an hour later, we lounged on the back patio in our pajamas with a fraction of a pitcher left. Aster was the easiest to get drunk because she rarely indulged in more than one glass of wine or cocktail in a week. She also had the body of a supermodel and those slender frames were great for catwalks, but not so great for holding liquor.

"How is Marley getting along at the Black Cloak Academy?" Aster asked. "Has she settled in?"

"Seems to be, thanks. She's always coming home with stories about this one's spell and that one's new cauldron." She also seemed to be making friends, which made my heart soar. Nothing made me happier than seeing my child happy.

"That's great," Linnea said. "If any child belongs in an academic setting, it's Marley. She and Bryn are similar in that way."

"Why don't you two flash your magic more often?" I asked.

"Flash our magic?" Aster echoed. "What does that even mean?"

"You're both so powerful, but you don't use it often," I said. "When I first met you, you were like some kind of superhero-supermodel hybrids bursting into my apartment to rescue us."

"I'm sure it seemed that way," Linnea said. "You'd never encountered magic before."

"Plus it was a dangerous situation," Aster added. "Lives were at stake. We had to act quickly."

"You have to remember that Mother was stunned when you were detected," Linnea said. "There was no time to assess. It was all systems go."

"I want the twins to be as capable without magic as with," Aster said. "That means leading by example."

"Is this your form of rebellion?" I asked. "Your mother is so hung up on legacies and power, maybe the two of you subconsciously turned away from magic as a result?"

Aster and Linnea stared into their glasses.

"I really like this drink," Aster said. "It doesn't even taste like alcohol."

"That's what makes it dangerous," I said. I didn't force the issue of their rebellion. This was meant to be a fun night with my cousins, not a therapy session.

Two and a half margaritas down the hatch and I was debating whether to confide in them about my research on Ivy. Apparently, my locked vault combination involved the word alcohol. It occurred to me that their mother might have told stories about Ivy over the years. After all, Ivy had been a High Priestess. Hyacinth would have shouted that one from the rooftops. It would be easy enough to make the inquiry seem nonchalant, especially when Marley was now the proud owner of both the wand and the grimoire. I took a deep breath and decided to test the waters.

"So, Marley keeps asking me all these questions about Ivy," I said.

"Ivy Cotton-Birch?" Aster asked, scrunching her nose. "What could she possibly want to know about her?"

"No, our ancestor," I replied. "Now that Marley has her wand and grimoire, she's fascinated by the history, only no one seems to know very much." I kept the discovery of the Book of Shadows to myself.

"That's what happens when there's a scandal," Aster said. "Suddenly everyone is ignorant or forgetful."

"That's certainly what happened with Wyatt," Linnea said. "Nobody wanted to know me once his antics became public knowledge. It was as though I'd been tainted by his behavior."

"Does it bother either of you that your mom gave the wand and grimoire to Marley instead of you or one of your kids?" I asked. Uh oh. It seemed that booze had greased the hinges for Operation Big Mouth.

Aster and Linnea exchanged glances. "Not me," Linnea said. "And it's certainly not a surprise that she didn't pass them to Bryn or Hudson. Not much my little werewolves could do with them."

"I don't even think I remembered that she had them," Aster said. "I don't know what she intended to do with them all these years, though. Let them collect dust in one of her cabinets?"

"That's true," I said. "It's not like she knew Marley and I would show up one day." She didn't even know that Marley existed until she appeared in Starry Hollow.

"She always hoped that you would," Linnea said. "She hated knowing that she had family out there with no way of finding you."

"Because she has control issues," I said. I swilled the rest of my margarita. "I think that bothered her more than anything. That someone was out from under her thumb."

"You're too hard on Mother," Aster said. "She only has our best interests at heart."

"So you don't know any details about Ivy?" I pressed.

"Mother was always somewhat tightlipped about her," Linnea said. "I remember doing a school project one year and asking for information on our ancestors. I thought it would be a simple request. You know how Mother is about the Rose family being so prominent."

I whistled. "I'm in touch with that particular obsession of hers."

Linnea smiled. "Yes, I guess you've gotten the blunt end of the Rose stick."

"According to your mother, I didn't get hit enough times with the Rose stick."

"Ember, don't be ridiculous," Aster said. "You're so pretty. Not everyone needs our signature hair color."

"Or your perfect features and unbelievable bodies." I downed another drink. "I mean, who needs all that when you can have stretch marks and dimples?"

Aster burped and then gasped at her own behavior.

"What's wrong with dimples?" Linnea asked. "Cheek dimples are adorable."

"Sure," I said. "The ones on your face, not the ones on your butt."

Linnea and Aster burst into uncontrollable laughter.

"Well, I can see who the lightweights are in this bunch," a familiar voice said. Wyatt Nash emerged from the shadows, followed by Bryn, Hudson, and...

"Granger?" His name escaped my lips before I could stop it.

"Evening, ladies," Wyatt said. "If I'd known there would be shenanigans happening here this evening, I would've hung around."

Linnea shot to her feet. "Wyatt Nash, what are you doing here at this hour with the children? They're supposed to be staying overnight with you." She shot her kids a guilty look. "No offense, you know I love you."

"That was the plan," Wyatt said lazily, "but it turns out that our presence has been requested at the Whitethorn tonight. I asked the kids whether they'd rather stay at my place on their own or come home and they chose to come home. What was I supposed to do about it?"

Linnea's cheeks flamed. "You are supposed to not go out tonight when you're in charge of our children."

"It's okay, Mom," Bryn said. "Even if he'd left us there, we probably would've made our way home anyway."

Linnea's eyes bulged. "That's not better! Wyatt, you can't just abandon your responsibilities whenever the wind blows in a different direction. You made an arrangement to have custody of your kids tonight. That means no Whitethorn. I don't care how busty the blonde was who invited you out. Her boobs will still be there tomorrow night."

"I'm not sure that they will," Wyatt said, completely serious. "Ariel is only in town tonight. She's on her way to Georgia for a conference. And she's got a friend for Granger."

I couldn't bring myself to meet the sheriff's gaze. I felt too awkward knowing that he was still on the prowl and that the Council of Elders were ready to oust him. I only hoped that he got his act together sooner rather than later before the repercussions were irreversible.

"I'm disappointed in you, Granger," Linnea said. "I expect this of Wyatt, but you're supposed to be the voice of reason here. How could you let this happen?"

"I'm not my brother's keeper," Granger replied evenly.

Linnea snorted. "Since when? You're always trying to get him to do the right thing. Now look at you. If you can't beat him, join him? Is that your new motto?"

"Ember, talk some sense into him," Aster urged, jostling my elbow.

Wyatt laughed loudly. "She's got no influence over him anymore, not since she ditched him for that walking corpse. Granger's shaken off her shackles and not a moment too soon. You break his heart, you don't get to be his moral compass. It doesn't work that way."

"No," I said, "but it doesn't mean he has to lose his way either. The Sheriff Nash I know doesn't need anyone to make him a better man. He already is one." This time I dared to look into Granger's deep brown eyes. For a fleeting moment, I thought I saw them soften, but they reverted back to two cold stones so quickly that I couldn't be certain.

"I'm tired," Hudson complained.

Linnea ruffled his hair. "You go on to bed, sweetheart. You, too, Bryn."

The teenagers disappeared into the house without another word.

"Sorry about crashing your party," Wyatt said.

"No, you're not," Linnea said, hands on hips. "As long as you get your way, you're happy."

Wyatt and Granger bumped fists.

"Enjoy the rest of your night, ladies," Wyatt said. "If any pillow fights erupt later, be sure to call me. I'd love to record it for posterity."

Linnea tossed the remnants of her glass at him but missed. He chuckled and swaggered away with Granger beside him.

"You look beautiful, Linnea," Wyatt called over his shoulder. "If I hadn't already been married to you, I'd be very interested."

"Thank the gods for men like Rick," Linnea mumbled. "They restore my faith in the male gender." She blew out a breath. "I used to say that about Granger, too. I have no idea what's gotten into him."

I stayed quiet on that subject, recognizing that I was drunk enough to spill the beans about the Council of Elders. I didn't want to betray Granger. The fewer residents that knew, the better.

"He certainly didn't seem like himself," Aster agreed. "Then again, my judgment is skewed. I'm so drunk now, I think I'd be willing to make out with that tree." She motioned to a fixture in the yard.

"That's not a tree," Linnea said. "That's a birdhouse."

We collapsed in peals of laughter.

CHAPTER TEN

DEPUTY BOLAN and I stood outside the entrance to Quicksilver. "Why don't you let me handle this one?" I asked.

The leprechaun looked at me askance. "You think because they sell broomsticks that I won't know how to conduct an interrogation? Do you know how law enforcement operates?"

"Sometimes?" Back in New Jersey, my closest interaction with law enforcement had been a parking ticket, so my frequent interactions with the sheriff's office in Starry Hollow was still a relatively new experience for me.

The deputy angled his head toward the door. "We're working this case together, remember? This isn't about proving ourselves. This is about solving the case so that the sheriff doesn't lose his job."

"I know," I said, sounding just a smidge like a teenager who was just told that she couldn't claim the child discount at the movie theater.

Deputy Bolan opened the door. "Civilians first."

I entered Quicksilver and was immediately set upon by a sales clerk.

"Stars and stones, if it isn't Ember Rose."

"You know me?" I didn't recognize him.

"How could I not?" He clapped merrily. "I would never want to disappoint a member of your family. You're far too important to our community."

"Thank you, Mr..." He was so intent on impressing me that I didn't have the heart to tell him that I wasn't here to make a purchase.

"Apple-White," he said. "Brock Apple-White."

"Well, Mr. Apple-White, I can assure you that my family is no more important than anyone else's," I said.

The wizard waved a hand. "Oh, please. Your family is full of influencers in this town. I follow Aster and Florian on social media. I love living vicariously through them."

Aster and Florian were active on social media? Why wasn't I in the loop?

"I hate to break it to you," Deputy Bolan said, "but Ms. Rose and I are here on official business."

His eyes widened. "Is this about that faulty broomstick that Evan Wormwood bought last week? Because I told him it was a manufacturing issue and that I would take care of it."

"No," I said. "This is about Shayna Masters."

The wizard's expression clouded over. "The tragedy. Shayna was far too vibrant to be taken from us so soon."

"You don't have to pretend with us," I said. "Obviously, the deputy here knows all about the police report you filed a couple weeks ago."

The wizard's shoulders sagged. "It wasn't personal," he insisted. "It was just that she could have killed someone, not to mention the fact that she caused damage to my shop that she refused to compensate me for." He pointed to the top of the shared wall between their shops. "You can see the spackle where I had to make the repair."

"Why don't you tell us exactly what happened?" I asked.

The wizard turned to the deputy. "It's all in my report that I gave to the sheriff."

"The report is very brief," the deputy said. "It would be helpful to hear the story in your own words."

"It was around noon that Tuesday," he said. "I remember it distinctly because I always eat my lunch at twelve and I'd just sat down at the counter and opened my tuna fish sandwich."

I cringed. "Tell me you have a fridge in the back room."

"Why would I need that?" he asked. "I bring a bottle of water and a sandwich every day."

"I know, but you bring tuna. First of all, fish always smells. Second of all, don't you put mayo on that sandwich? Then you leave it out for hours before you eat it?" Gross.

He gave me an innocent look. "What? I've never been sick from it."

"Consider yourself lucky," I replied.

"Can we stop criticizing his life choices and get back to the subject at hand?" Deputy Bolan asked in an impatient tone.

"I don't know that I was judging him as much as I was trying to be a helper," I said.

"Zip it, Rose," the leprechaun said.

"Anyway, I'd just taken my first bite of the sandwich when I heard a strange popping sound coming from next door. Next thing I knew, a small object burst through the wall where I showed you and landed in aisle three. I went over to investigate and discovered a bullet embedded in one of my most expensive broomsticks. I'd never even seen a bullet before, but I knew it looked dangerous. Turns out it was silver. If I'd had a werewolf in here, it could have been disastrous."

"If anyone had been hit by that bullet, it would have been disastrous," the deputy said. "It's just that normal bullets wouldn't kill a werewolf, but any bullet could kill us."

I cocked my head at the leprechaun. "Are you sure about that? Maybe we should test it out. Could be that you're more resilient than you think." I fluttered my eyelashes at him and he scowled.

"So you went to confront Shayna?" the deputy asked.

"You bet your sweet bippy I did," the wizard said heatedly. "I was ready to whip out my wand. I carried the damaged broomstick over with the bullet still in it. When I entered the shop, Shayna was standing there with a pistol in each hand. One of them was still smoking."

"What did she say when you told her what happened?" I asked.

"She was excited," he replied. "Can you believe that? I was so upset that I was shaking and I told her that I could have been killed and that there was damage. All she could talk about was the fact that the pistols worked, which meant she could sell them for a higher price."

"Did you ask for compensation?" I asked.

"Of course," he said. "I even took her to show her the damage. I also showed her the cost of the damaged broomstick." He shook his head. "She said it was an accident and that my insurance would cover it. I told her I was going to go to the sheriff and she blew it off like it was no big deal."

"Couldn't the sheriff have charged her with illegal possession of a firearm or something?" I asked, directing the question to Deputy Bolan.

"We don't actually have a law on the books regarding guns," the deputy said. "They're not really a paranormal object. That's why they were probably so valuable to Shayna. You don't see pistols of any kind in Starry Hollow, let alone ones with silver bullets."

"She said they were antique and reportedly used to kill

some famous werewolf back in the 1800s," the wizard said. "She gave me the whole story because she was so excited. She didn't care at all about me or my shop. I think she might have been issued a fine by Sheriff Nash, but she made so much money that it wasn't any kind of punishment to her."

The deputy nodded. "She did pay a fine in connection with a reckless endangerment charge. Did you consider a lawsuit?"

The wizard grimaced. "Believe me, I thought about it, but it seems like it would serve only the lawyers and neither of us. It would've been better if she'd made things right from the start."

"What has your relationship been with her since then?" I asked. "Were you on speaking terms?"

"If I saw her, I turned away," he said. "It was only two weeks ago. The whole thing still feels too raw and the fact that she never showed any remorse…" He dropped his gaze. "I mean, it's horrible that she's dead, but I'm not going to lose any sleep over it."

"Mr. Apple-White, where were you from late afternoon to evening on Saturday?" Deputy Bolan asked.

The wizard appeared thoughtful. "I was still here. We close at six on Saturdays and then I stay another hour to do admin."

"Can anyone confirm your whereabouts?" the deputy asked.

The wizard blinked. "You don't really think I had anything to do with her death, do you?"

"We have to cover all our bases," the deputy said. "If you have an alibi, that just makes our job easier."

The wizard frowned. "Why is it your job anyway? A murder case is a pretty big deal. Shouldn't Sheriff Nash be handling this?"

"Oh, he is," I said quickly. "We're just investigating the second-tier suspects, of which you are one."

The wizard seemed heartened by this. "Well, that's a relief. I *would* lose sleep at night if I thought people suspected me of murder. That's horrible." He went behind the counter and opened a drawer. "I have a log of receipts with customer names from Saturday. You're more than welcome to contact the ones time-stamped Saturday and confirm that I was here." He produced a folder and handed it to Deputy Bolan. "You can also check my social media accounts. I was pretty active that evening. I posted a few photos of new inventory. I use Quicksilver as a handle and a hashtag."

"Thank you very much for this," the leprechaun said. "I'll make copies for our file and get these back to you."

"No need," the wizard said. "These are actually my backup copies. I keep the main set on the computer."

"Perfect," the deputy said, and tucked the file under his arm.

The wizard shifted his attention to me. "Are you sure I can't interest you in a new broomstick for you or your daughter? I'd love to post a photo of you riding one of our deluxe broomsticks. I can offer you a discount."

"No, but thank you," I said. "I have a relatively new broomstick that my boyfriend bought for me and my daughter really doesn't like to fly." Marley's anxiety kicked into high gear when it came to heights.

"How about that?" the wizard said. "Must be inherited from another side of the family. Was her father a wizard?"

I didn't really want to discuss Marley's human father with the random wizard in Quicksilver. "Thank you for your time," I said, ignoring his question. "Be sure not to leave town until we've cleared you. Standard procedure."

"No problem there," he said. "My schedule doesn't allow for another vacation until at least seven months from now.

That's one of the reasons I enjoy social media so much. I get to see all the fun everyone else is having." He heaved a regretful sigh.

"All that glitters isn't gold, Mr. Apple-White," I said. "Half of them are secretly miserable and the other half are probably using digital manipulation."

The wizard appeared stricken. "Really?"

The leprechaun shook his head at me. "Congratulations, Rose, you've given him a new tagline for the shop's social media accounts," the deputy said. "Quicksilver—where dreams come to die."

CHAPTER ELEVEN

"Can we have all my lessons in your warehouse?" I asked. "That place is far more interesting than a clearing in the woods."

The Master of Incantation gave me a wry smile. "Firstly, it's a workshop, not a warehouse. I'm not storing goods. Secondly, that's my personal space. I prefer to preserve it as my sanctuary. It's where I go to get away."

"But not for me," I said. "You can't possibly need to seek sanctuary from this." I pointed my wand at my face and drew a circle in the air.

Wren chuckled. "You're an interesting mix of anxiety and arrogance, I'll give you that."

"I don't suppose there's a market for a potion like that."

"Why don't we get started? We have a number of incantations to get through today."

"What's your hurry? Hot date with Delphine?" Wren had been quietly dating Delphine Winter, a witch and local librarian. She'd briefly dated Florian, but my cousin simply wasn't prepared for a serious relationship.

"I see what you're doing," the handsome wizard said.

"What? I'm standing here waiting for my lesson, ready to absorb all your wisdom."

"Nice try. You're trying to distract me from the lesson with personal questions." He wagged a wand at me. "I'm onto your tricks, you know."

"They're really not tricks," I replied. "I'm simply making conversation. Getting to know you better. I really like Delphine and I want to see her happy."

"Delphine and I are doing really well. We appreciate your interest, but why don't we get back to business?"

I eyed him closely. "Why don't you want to talk about her more? Is there a problem? I sense reluctance."

He shot me a warning glance. "Today we're going to cover one of my favorite spells, so I suggest you pay attention."

I laughed. "That's adorable that you have a favorite spell. How about a favorite color? I bet you have one of those, too."

"Of course I do. I'm not a monster."

"Aren't you going to tell me what it is?" I tilted my head, studying him. "I bet it's blue."

"Actually, it's green," he said smugly. "Now, about this spell..." He lifted his wand.

"Is your favorite spell written in your Book of Shadows?" I honestly wasn't trying to divert his attention this time. I was genuinely curious.

Wren lowered his wand. "As a matter fact, I do. I have an entire section of the book devoted to favorite spells."

"What else do you have in yours?"

He exhaled in frustration. "Ember..."

I zigzagged my wand through the air. "I swear I'm not trying to get out of my lesson. I'm genuinely interested. Lee has me making my own and I'm struggling to decide what to include. I don't really have favorites yet. What else do you have?" Maybe Ivy would have similar content in hers.

He slipped his wand through a loop on his belt and

stuffed his hands into his cloak pockets. "The book is really personal to the witch or wizard. The things I include in mine aren't necessarily what you would choose to include in yours."

"I get that, but I'm curious what you think is important enough to be included in yours. Would you be upset if somebody looked through it? Is it that kind of personal?" I was curious as to whether Ivy's book was warded because she had secrets to keep or simply because she didn't want anyone to have such an intimate look at her. It would be like glimpsing someone's soul. I knew that would make me uncomfortable, so maybe the same was true for Ivy.

"I guess I'm a somewhat private wizard," Wren said. "My brother has seen my book loads of times, but I'd probably be annoyed if some random witch or wizard started flipping through it. I haven't even shown Delphine."

"Do you ward yours?"

He chuckled. "Maybe I did when I was a teenager, but I don't now. It's not that I have anything to hide. When I die, there's nothing in it to embarrass or humiliate me."

"Well, thanks for the heads up. That's already a disappointment."

"These questions are awfully specific, Ember. Are you planning to record all of your deepest, darkest secrets in your Book of Shadows? Because now I'm intrigued."

"I'm just not very good at sharing and I was getting the sense that I would have to put a lot of myself into the book. I like all the pieces of me to be intact rather than hidden away in a book."

"Understood." He retrieved his wand. "Let's get started or we'll never finish." He raised his wand, ready for action.

"What about a spell to capture negative energy?" I blurted.

His arm dropped to his side. "Why would you want to

capture it? That's typically the kind of energy you want to let go of."

I began to pace the ground in front of him. "Remember when you tried to cleanse Ivy's wand and you said there was negative energy trapped in it? I think her Book of Shadows has some kind of resistance magic attached to it, too."

"You have her Book of Shadows, too? How'd you manage that?"

Oops. "I may have found her BOS buried in the garden of the cottage."

His mouth curved slightly upward. "Her BOS?"

"Makes it sound more professional when you create abbreviations," I said with an air of authority.

"I'll take your word for it." He rubbed his square jawline. "Why would she bury her…BOS in the garden?"

"Maybe she didn't. Maybe someone else did. It's warded to the hilt, I can tell you that much."

"What does Hyacinth think?" he asked.

Guilt saturated my veins. "I'm keeping this one on the DL."

"That doesn't make you sound professional," he said. "That makes you sound unhip." He folded his arms. "Why are you keeping it a secret from her? You've discovered a family heirloom on her property."

"Technically, it's my property, but I digress." I struggled to choose my words carefully. "I can't explain it, but I would prefer to keep this quiet for now until I learn more."

"Learn what exactly?"

"Who buried it and why? Why is it warded? Why is the energy so powerful? Why does the wand feel like a volcano on the verge of eruption?"

"I would think your aunt is the perfect witch to assist you with those questions. Last time I checked she was the most powerful witch in town."

I pointed a finger at him. "Promise you'll keep this a secret. Please." I saw the flash of hesitation in his eyes. I understood. Nobody liked to be on the wrong side of Hyacinth Rose-Muldoon. "Some part of me wonders whether she has an ulterior motive in giving Ivy's wand to Marley, so I'd like to figure out more of her story before I involve my aunt. I feel like she knows more than she's sharing and there must be a reason for it. The Book of Shadows might yield those answers." If I could crack it open.

Wren offered a reassuring nod. "Okay, Ember. I won't breathe a word, not even to Delphine."

"I'm sorry to put you in that position," I said. "I know it's not ideal, but I trust you. I need wizardly help and Gandalf isn't available."

"He's your first choice for wizardly help, huh?"

"Dude, he's everybody's first choice for wizardly help."

He arched an eyebrow. "Not Dumbledore?"

"He'd be my second choice."

Wren raised two fingers in a V. "I solemnly swear to keep any and all secrets shared with me by Ember Rose in the proverbial vault." He twisted an imaginary lock in front of his mouth.

"Is that an actual oath?"

"No, but I do swear." He paused. "How about a high-five to seal the deal?"

"Good enough for me." And we slapped hands.

"I do know a few spells that can trap negative energy," he said. "They're not common, but they exist."

"I'm wondering if they're used as a way of protecting the outside world," I said. "Trap the negative energy in one place so that it can't spread and impact anyone."

"Could be."

Another idea occurred to me. "What about an incantation that breaks through a false persona?"

Wren blinked. "Okay, how did we jump from Ivy's negative energy to this?"

I tapped my head. "Sorry, that's the way this noggin bounces." Actually, it was the mention of Aunt Hyacinth, which led me to Craig and his smooth facade. "If someone is putting on a front, is there a spell I can do to see past it?"

"There's always a spell if you're creative enough. That's the beauty of magic." Wren dragged a hand through his thick hair, thinking. "You could try a mind reading spell, an aura spell that might reveal his true intentions, or even a reverse illusion spell."

"A reverse illusion?"

"Like if someone is pretending to be a sweet fairy, but it turns out they're a mischievous goblin, you'll be able to see through their illusion. That sort of thing."

"Hmm." Could Craig be another creature entirely? He was Linden's cousin so it seemed unlikely. "Can you teach me the aura spell?"

"You know what? It isn't what I had planned for today, but the fact that you're eager to learn any spell is good enough for me." He pushed up his cloak sleeves. "If you don't want the object of the spell to know what you're up to, you need to find a subtle way to aim your wand at them."

"Subtle is my middle name," I said.

"You're from New Jersey. You don't have a subtle bone in your body."

"Fair enough, but I'm good at sneaking." Which definitely played a role in my teen pregnancy. If I hadn't been so good at sneaking out with Karl, I wouldn't have Marley, so that was a huge win as far as I was concerned.

"You're going to place your feet shoulder-with apart." He demonstrated the stance for me.

"That's not subtle. If I stand like that, then there's no

chance to sneak. I'm basically announcing I'm about to do something magical."

Wren rolled his eyes. "Just follow my lead for once."

I stood beside him and copied his pose.

"Focus your will," he said. "Feel the energy flow from your body to the wand, which is simply an extension of you."

"I know all this."

"Yes, but you need practice. Knowing and implementing are two different skills."

He made a good point. I drew a cleansing breath and focused on the energy whirling inside me. Then I tried to steer the pulsing energy to the wand in my hand. "It's like trying to herd talking raccoons," I said.

"That's your energy, Ember. It's wild. You need to work on taming it."

I concentrated on pulling the energy into a compact ball and pushing it toward my wand. "Now what?"

"Aim your wand at me and say…"

I shook my head. "No, this won't work." Craig would be on to me in a heartbeat.

"Once you master the spell, you can finesse it so that it's almost undetectable."

"We're talking about me, Wren. That could take years. How about the mind reading one?"

"Maybe you should let Marigold do that?" he replied. "She's the Mistress of Psychic Skills."

"Yes, but her lessons aren't geared toward this kind of thing." Plus, she might rat me out to Hyacinth, who wouldn't take kindly to her niece undermining her seemingly perfect suitor.

"Fine. You basically do the spell on yourself with this one so that you can read the minds in your immediate vicinity."

"That's better."

He rested the tip of his wand against his temple and said, "Repeat after me. *Mentis lector.*"

I copied his movement and said, "*Mentis lector.*"

Can you hear me? Wren asked.

"Of course I can. You're standing right next to me. I can also smell that you ate garlic...Oh."

Wren grinned. *If you caught me unaware, you'd be able to hear my thoughts at this precise moment. That's what you're after, isn't it?*

"Sure is." And I could finally decide whether Craig was friend or foe. "You're like a taller, square-jawed version of Raoul now."

Gee, thanks.

"His hair is more lustrous, though." I tucked away my wand. "How long will the spell last?"

This one is basic, so not very long, Wren said. *If you ask the right questions or make the right comments, you should be able to hear their thoughts and hopefully get what you need.*

My brain starting click away. "Man, this spell could be invaluable." Adolescent daughter. Withholding boyfriend. Secretive aunt. The possibilities were endless.

And also dangerous, Wren said pointedly. *Sometimes ignorance is bliss.*

"I'll let your librarian girlfriend know you said that...in your head."

He bit back a smile and continued, *But if you have a specific need to see whether someone is genuine, this might be a quick and reasonable way to handle it.*

"More like down and dirty, but I'm sold. Thanks for the lesson, Wren. I appreciate your willingness to indulge me."

"Whatever it takes," he said, reverting back to the spoken word. "I know you think you're not as skilled as the other members of your family, but I still think you're packed with potential."

"The only thing I'm packed with is all the extra cheese I've been eating," I countered. "On that note, have you ever tried pimento cheese? I'm a recent convert."

"I try to avoid dairy. It upsets my stomach." An idea seemed to occur to him. "Just out of curiosity, have you talked to Magnus about any of this?"

"Magnus Destry? Why?" I didn't have much interaction with the High Priest.

"If you're looking to dig for information and keep your aunt in the dark, he's probably a good wizard to turn to," he said cryptically.

I leaned forward. "Really? Do tell."

"I'm only spitballing here, but I've always gotten the sense that Magnus resents your family's influence and the whole One True Witch connection."

"Then why would he help me? I'm still a member of the family."

Wren started to laugh but then seemed to think better of it. "Of course you are, but I think Magnus recognizes that you and Marley are…different."

I gave him the stink eye. "I'll choose to take that as a compliment."

Wren clapped me on the back. "Good luck with your spy mission, Ember, and, if anyone catches you reading minds, you didn't learn it from me."

"That won't take much convincing. Everybody already knows I don't learn anything from you," I said, and raced out of the clearing before he could hex me.

CHAPTER TWELVE

DEPUTY BOLAN and I decided to split the customer list in half that Lois had given us in order to expedite matters. I'd received another not-so-anonymous note from Arthur Rutledge to indicate that the elders were getting restless. It seemed a bit unnecessary given that we had a deadline already but, apparently, Sheriff Nash's wolfish alter ego had struck again at Glitter Me This and more complaints had rolled in to the council. Someone needed to put a leash on that guy before he made matters worse.

"Do you want to come with me today?" I asked Alec. The vampire stood at the stove making his version of a frittata.

"Are you conducting more interviews?" he asked.

"I'm going to knock out two of them today. One of them is just a courtesy call, though. I have to let her know that her brooch is now in evidence and won't be for sale at Beswitched. Kind of awkward really because Shayna probably shouldn't have been wearing it in the first place."

"Sounds like you can handle it on your own," Alec said. "We both know you're more than capable."

"You might want to consider jumping in on the second one," I said. "I need to go see somebody at Elixir." I cocked an eyebrow. "Care to go for a drink this evening, Mr. Hale?"

His expression reflected pure desire. "Why do I find it so irresistible when you address me by my formal name? You have quite a strange effect on me, Ms. Rose."

I smiled. "Strange—or amazing?"

He served the frittata onto two plates. "How about amazingly strange?"

"When you make food like this, it can be whatever you want." I pushed back my chair. "I need ketchup."

He blocked my path to the refrigerator. "For what?"

"For flavor," I said. "I always put ketchup on eggs."

"These are no mere eggs. This is a frittata, and I can assure you that my frittata does not require any condiments. It's already bursting with flavor."

I wrapped my arms around his trim waist. "You know what else is bursting with flavor?"

His fangs descended. "Don't tempt me now. The frittatas will get cold."

"And my frittatas are in danger of getting cold if you don't warm them up with those strong hands of yours, Mr. Hale." I dragged out his name in my lowest, sexiest voice, which probably sounded more like Darth Vader than the seductive one in my head.

Alec pulled me flat against his chest and kissed me with an intensity usually reserved for drunken nights in the Whitethorn parking lot.

"Why, Alec," I said, pulling back slightly. "You're really loosening up."

He pressed his forehead against mine. "How loose would you like to see me?"

I splayed my hands against his firm chest. "You know

what the therapist said. No full-on sexy times until we've established a stronger foundation. If we want to give this relationship its best chance, we have to put in the work first."

He stole another quick kiss before turning back to his frittata. "You're quite right, and I very much do want this relationship to work."

"So you're cool with ketchup now?"

"As though I would ever presume to tell you what or how to eat."

"Phew," I said. "I thought we were going to have to end things right here and now. Ketchup is definitely a hill I'm willing to die on." I went to the refrigerator and retrieved the bottle.

"I'm going to leave the courtesy call to you, but I would be more than happy to escort you to Elixir tonight," he said. "Although I can't promise that I won't try to lure you into a dark corner and have my way with you."

Heat coiled in my stomach at the thought. "Don't make promises you can't keep." I shook off the sexy vibe. "I've decided to take my broomstick to see Sonja Brickstone."

The vampire perked up. "Your broomstick? What prompted this?"

"I haven't been using it as much as I should. I love to fly. I only tend not to because of Marley, but there's no reason I can't use one when she's not around." I shoveled down a forkful of frittata. "Besides, this broomstick is special. I should be using it more often."

His fork hovered midway between the plate and his mouth. "Oh? Why is that?"

"Because someone special bought it for me." I met his gaze across the table.

"Perhaps you should give him something special in return as a thank you," Alec suggested.

I pointed the fork at him. "You realize that's bordering on prostitution."

"Certainly not when there's been such a lag between the original gift and the later payment."

Great Goddess. The sexual tension was too much to bear sometimes. Part of me wanted to take him right there on the table, but I knew that wasn't the smart play. The therapist was right. Waiting was best for a healthy relationship. We both had issues to work through. My issue with guilt was at the forefront right now, which was why I finished my frittata and rode straight over to Sonja Brickstone's house.

Sonja lived in a beautiful three-story house not far from the row of Painted Pixies. The architecture would have looked equally at home in New Orleans with its double balconies and intricate wrought iron design. The front door was painted a glossy black with shutters to match.

I knocked on the door and was greeted by one of the tallest women I'd ever seen. She wore an elegant, floor-length dress that seemed more appropriate for an evening out than the middle of the day. Then again, I was someone who was more than happy to go to the grocery store in pajamas if I could get away with it.

"Hi there. Are you Sonja Brickstone?"

She peered down her patrician nose at me. "That's right. And you are?"

"Ember Rose," I said. "I'm writing an article for the paper about Shayna Masters and was wondering if you might have a minute. I understand that you were one of her best customers."

Sonja placed a hand over her heart. "I was so distressed when I heard the news. Shayna was more than a light in my life. She was an eternal flame." She stepped back to allow me entry. "Please come in. May I offer you a glass of white wine?"

"No, thank you," I said. "Not while I'm working." Deputy Bolan and I had agreed that I would use the newspaper as a cover story when I interviewed paranormals without him, which made breaking the news about the brooch awkward but still doable.

"I still have a hard time believing she's gone," Sonja said. "I think it's going to take some time to process." She sashayed into the formal living room and sat on the Chippendale loveseat. She gestured for me to sit in the Stickley chair opposite her.

"I understand you frequently brought her items for resale," I said. "Do you plan to leave them at Be-switched and hope that Lois can sell them or will you take them back?"

Sonja's polite smile melted away. "I'm not even thinking about that right now. My heart breaks for Franco and Lois. I sent them each a condolence card, but as soon as they're ready to receive visitors, I'll be there."

"That's very kind of you," I said. "There's one item I need to address with you that might be upsetting."

"I highly doubt it. Nothing's rattled me since my divorce from that mama's boy," Sonja said bitterly. "On the upside, it helped me become the Amazon I was always meant to be."

Let's see how hardened she really was. "According to the police report, Shayna choked on a brooch and, sadly, that's what killed her."

Sonja gasped. "My word. How would such a thing even happen?"

"She was wearing the brooch at the wedding," I explained. "The police believe that the killer may have forced it down her throat in a heated moment."

Sonja blanched. "Heated? More like violent and monstrous. I truly hope Sheriff Nash and his deputy are making every effort to apprehend this vile creature."

"Everything that can be done is being done," I assured her. No need to mention the current crisis with Sheriff Nash. "The reason I'm even sharing this information is because the brooch belonged to you. It was the flower with different colored gemstones."

Her mouth dropped open and she took a moment to recover. "I beg your pardon. Are you telling me that the brooch I brought her to resell at Be-switched is the same brooch that was used to murder her?"

"Apparently, Shayna sometimes liked to wear items from the shop as a way of showing them off to potential customers," I said. "She wore the brooch to the wedding because she knew she would get a lot of eyes on it and increase its chances of being sold."

Sonja's brow furrowed. "Yes, yes. I was aware that she did that. I'm just floored that my little brooch is what killed her." She pressed her palms flat against her cheeks. "I think I'll be needing that glass of wine now."

"I'm sorry to be the one to tell you," I said. "I know from the deputy that they'll need to keep the brooch in evidence, so you won't be able to sell it."

She swatted a hand in the air. "Oh my goodness. Don't give it another thought. It's just a thing. It had been sitting in my jewelry box for ages collecting dust." Her hand moved to cover her stomach. "I feel quite ill."

"I'm sorry," I said.

"Whatever you write in that article on Shayna, please be sure to mention that Sonja Brickstone thought the world of her. And you can quote me on that." She held a pillow against her stomach. "I'm sure you've already heard a number of negative stories about her, but I only saw her good side. I'd like to make sure the record reflects that not everyone found her to be difficult or challenging. I suppose Franco will say the same, though. Still, two positive voices are better than one."

"Three, with Lois," I said.

Sonja pressed her lips together and nodded vigorously. "Shayna was more than helpful to me after my divorce. I was desperate for money at the time because my accounts were frozen during the proceedings. My ex-husband is a class A wereass, you see. Spent more time on the croquet court than in our bedroom because those were the only balls he was comfortable with. Technically, I wasn't supposed to sell any of my belongings until a settlement was reached, but I didn't have a choice. I wouldn't have been able to pay my bills. Shayna told me not to worry, that she would sell every piece she possibly could."

"And did she?"

Sonja nodded. "That's why I continue to bring her pieces to this day. I no longer need the money, thank the gods, but I'm happy to give her my business. Anytime I come across something that I no longer need or want, I pass it along to Be-switched, like the brooch."

"And you get a cut of the sale price, right?"

"I do, but I donate my portion to charity. I'm very involved with the Amazon Orphan Society."

A-ha! No wonder Sonja was so tall. "My family is involved with a few nonprofits, too. I'm on the board of the Rose Foundation."

She stared at me. "Wait, you're a Rose?" She scrutinized me. "I suppose I should've realized when you introduced yourself, but you…"

"I know, I know. I don't have the telltale hair or the perfect body."

"I know your cousins in passing," she said. "Aster and I have attended many of the same charitable events together."

"Yes, she and Sterling definitely attend a lot of those."

"If you're hungry, I can have my chef whip up a quick cheese board."

"Thanks, but I have to get home." I didn't want to say for a runecraft lesson because that sounded lame, even in my head.

Sonja stood and smoothed the front of her dress. "Well, if there's anything you need from me—anything at all—please feel free to contact me. I'm more than happy to help. I won't have a sound night's sleep until this monster is caught."

"Thank you so much," I said. "And I'm really sorry about the brooch. I know it's not the kind of news you want to hear."

She blinked away tears. "I just feel so guilty that it was my piece that she happened to be wearing that day. If she'd been wearing a statement necklace or chunky earrings…" She trailed off. "It doesn't bear thinking about."

"I know it's hard, but try not to blame yourself."

She accompanied me to the door. "When do you think the article will be published?"

"Uh, next week?" Assuming I managed to actually write one.

"I'll be sure to keep an eye out for it." Her gaze lingered on me. "You know, if you ever want any fashion tips, I'm very generous with advice. Maybe you could include a column in the paper detailing our discussion."

I wasn't sure how to respond. "That's nice of you." Or maybe rude. I couldn't decide. "I'll mention it to my boss." Not.

"Have you considered thinning your eyebrows just a hair, no pun intended?" She laughed awkwardly.

I clenched my hands into fists. "Never. Apparently, the One True Witch had caterpillar-style eyebrows, so I've been forbidden from touching them. They think it's where my magic resides." A little lie inspired by…a story from the Bible.

Minotaur shit. I was going straight to Hell courtesy of Samson and Delilah.

Her brow lifted. "You must be *very* powerful."

"You have no idea," I said, and forced myself back to my broomstick before I did something I'd regret.

CHAPTER THIRTEEN

Thankfully, I arrived at the cottage in time for my lesson with Hazel. Twice in one week wasn't my idea of fun, but I'd managed to derail her last time, so it was only fair.

"Your aunt has requested that we take this show on the road," Hazel announced.

"Wow, big day. You're finally acknowledging that this is a circus and you're the head clown." With her curly red hair, pink cheeks, and demonic expression, she was always a crazed clown to me.

Hazel glared at me. "Her Majesty has requested a demonstration of your progress."

"My progress with runecraft?" I scrunched my nose. "Is she set on disappointment or what?"

"I think she's trying to impress her new beau," Hazel said, lowering her voice.

"Why are you whispering?" I asked. "Aunt Hyacinth isn't here."

"I don't know, actually. It just seems polite to speak softly with regard to your aunt's suitors."

"At her age, we should be shouting it from the rooftops," I said. "If you've got it, flaunt it."

Hazel bristled. "At her age? You'd better mind your tongue, young witch. I know more than a few spells that will paralyze it. It would be a nice change for all of us."

I gave her a pointed look. "I can think of a powerful vampire who might object."

Hazel cringed. "No need for details on your romantic interactions with Mr. Hale, thank you."

"Are you sure? It might save you the trouble of reading that bodice ripper in your bottomless bag."

Hazel pulled the bag close to her chest. "Since when do you have some kind of X-ray vision?"

I tipped back my head and laughed. "That's not X-ray vision. That's called knowing your mark."

Hazel's eyes narrowed to slits. "It's not a bodice ripper, I'll have you know. It's women's fiction."

"Is there a dude on the cover with his chest exposed and a woman in the throes of passion?"

Hazel slowly slid the bag under her chair. "Maybe," she mumbled.

"Hazel, there's nothing wrong with reading romance. If you love it, you need to own it, not be embarrassed."

"I know it's pure fantasy, but there's something to be said for a gent with rippling muscles and the patience of a saint." She shuddered with pleasure.

I held up a hand. "Okay, now it's my turn to be grossed out. I don't need the details of your imaginary sex life." I had no doubt circus porn was a fetish I hadn't been exposed to yet and I was grateful for it.

"I know you prefer the epic fantasies that Mr. Hale writes, but I've always been partial to hunky Scots in kilts."

"Oh, you prefer historical romance. Even better."

She shook a finger at me. "If you tell anyone, you will live to regret it."

"Hazel, I'm telling you not to be ashamed. I don't judge anyone's reading choices. I think it's great that there are books that resonate with you. To be honest, I don't even like epic fantasy. I only read them because Alec wrote them and it's an opportunity to see inside his head."

She examined me. "Is that true?"

I held up a hand. "Swear. Marley's the real fan."

"And what do you like to read?"

I flashed a smile. "Runecraft, of course."

She looked for something to throw at me but came up empty-handed.

"How am I supposed to show off my rune skills anyway?" I asked. "It's pretty much the worst subject she could possibly choose."

Hazel hoisted her tote bag over her shoulder. "Quit bellyaching and let's get on with it. You're worse than a toddler who's been told she can't have dessert."

I scoffed. "No, I'm much louder when it comes to dessert deprivation." I glanced around the table. "Do I bring the BBOS? I'll need a crutch."

Hazel leveled me with a look. "Right. Wren mentioned your attempts to abbreviate our terminology."

"You guys talk about me when I'm not around?" That revelation managed to be both flattering and annoying.

"It's hard not to, Ember."

I suddenly remembered that I'd sworn him to secrecy about Ivy's Book of Shadows. "What else did he say?"

She gave me a curious look. "Why does that matter?"

I shrugged. "Because I want to be liked."

She barked a short laugh. "Since when?"

"Okay, fine. I'm nosy and vaguely narcissistic."

"That's more like it. He said he's pleased that you're

beginning to think more independently instead of simply following along with the lesson plan."

"That's it? Nothing else?"

"That's a pretty high compliment from Wren. Isn't that enough for you?"

It was. "Lead on, ringmaster. Our audience awaits."

Hazel and I flew the short distance to Thornhold on our broomsticks to find Aunt Hyacinth on the veranda, engaged in conversation with Craig and Florian. By the time we landed on the lawn and joined them, Simon was in the process of distributing drinks and a plate of cookies.

"Craig, what a nice surprise. Again," I said. And the perfect opportunity to test my mind reading skills. "No Linden?"

"Lovely to see you again, Ember," he said. "No, I'm afraid my cousin had an appointment. She'll be sorry to have missed this. I understand you'll be regaling us with your considerable talents this afternoon."

Hazel choked back a laugh.

"Anything else I can bring for you?" Simon asked, directing the question to my aunt.

I raised my hand. "Ooh, make mine an eyebright and tonic, please."

"Since when do you drink those?" Florian asked.

"I'm trying to expand my horizons," I replied.

"I did that last night," my cousin said, suggestively wiggling his eyebrows. "Several times, in fact."

"Florian, please," my aunt said.

"That's what she said." Florian laughed. Sometimes he was awesome and other times...Well, he was this guy.

"Who's the unlucky lady?" I asked. Florian would be sure to crush her heart and blend it with his kale and chickweed smoothie by tomorrow.

"A gentleman never tells," he said vaguely.

"Which means you don't want me to know. Interesting." Well, I knew it wasn't Delphine because she and Wren were still going strong. "Do you know, Simon?"

The servant avoided my gaze. "What Master Florian does in his own home is his business."

Ooh, Simon definitely knew! The reasons to cast the mind reading spell had grown exponentially since my arrival.

Precious, my aunt's familiar, darted between my legs to climb on Hyacinth's lap and dip her tongue into the cocktail. Gross. The longhaired, white cat proved a bit too eager, causing my aunt to spill a few drops on her royal blue kaftan. The cat wasted no time trying to lick the fallen droplets as well. It seemed my aunt and her familiar shared a taste for alcohol the way Raoul and I shared a taste for pizza.

"If you'll excuse me for a moment," I said, "I need the bathroom."

"No escaping out the front door," Hazel hissed.

I dashed into the house and across the foyer to the powder room.

"Are you well, Miss Ember?" Simon asked, as I hurried past him. "Does something not agree with you?"

"Story of my life," I called over my shoulder. Once I was safely installed in the powder room, I took out my wand and focused on corralling my energy. "*Mentis lector.*"

I ran the water and pretended to wash my hands in case anyone was listening because—let's face it—I was in my aunt's house and the paranoia was strong in me. I quickly returned to the veranda, ready to work my magic.

"Where is everyone?" I asked.

"Your aunt and Florian had to take an important call," Craig said. "Something to do with the foundation. Hazel and Simon went to the kitchen so that Hazel could show him how to make the drink she requested. It seems rather high-maintenance."

"Ha!" I said. This was perfect. It would be easier for me to try this without my aunt's critical gaze on me.

"You two have been spending a lot of time together," I said. "You must be really into each other." I listened intently for the words in his head rather than the ones he spoke.

"Hyacinth and I have certainly been enjoying each other's company," he said. "She's a remarkable witch. I feel fortunate to have met her."

His head was surprisingly silent. I decided to try again. Maybe I was too distracted by his oral response.

"Does it bother you that Zale is still sniffing around?" I asked. There. A mention of the competition might whip the brain into action.

Craig laughed lightly. "Hyacinth is a grown witch and can do as she pleases. If Zale is her preference, then I accept that." He leaned over and whispered, "Though I have to say that I get the distinct impression that I'm her preference these days. I can't pretend not to be chuffed."

Not a single thought while he spoke. That made no sense. I decided to stay quiet for a moment and see whether that triggered any thoughts I could read. Maybe if I did something…provocative.

I reached for a cookie and 'accidentally' knocked it to the floor. "I'm so clumsy sometimes." I stood and bent over, positioning my bottom directly in his line of sight. If the guy found kaftans sexy, I wasn't sure that I was his taste, but it was worth a try.

I lingered in this awkward position, listening for a single thought. None was forthcoming. This guy was either brain dead or blocking spells like mine. My money was on the latter.

"Ember, what in the Goddess of the Moon's name are you doing?" My aunt's voice snapped me back to reality and I promptly returned to my seat. *She can't possibly be trying to lure away my darling Craig. She's far too smitten with Alec.*

Well, at least I knew my spell worked.

"I dropped a cookie and Simon wasn't here to pick it up. You should really talk to him about slacking off. I know he's worked for you a long time, but you have to maintain standards." I was so nervous that I knew I was doomed to prattle unless I put a stop to it myself, so I shoved the cookie in my mouth.

"Are you…eating the cookie that fell on the floor?" Craig asked, aghast.

"Ten second rule," I said, still chewing.

"You'll have to forgive my niece," Aunt Hyacinth said. "She wasn't raised in Starry Hollow." *More like a barn in New Jersey. Do they even have barns in New Jersey? I suppose all the animals congregate together along the turnpike.*

Hmm. Still no thoughts in his head. He should at least be expressing internal mortification.

"Ember, you should have joined us on the call," Florian said, as he returned to the veranda. "There's a new organization that's interested in partnering with us." *And the woman spearheading it is hot, hot, hot.*

"You need to be careful not to spread your resources too thin," Craig interjected. "Your generosity is to be admired, but even great wealth has its limits."

Hyacinth smiled up at him. "Craig, I do appreciate your conservative attitude." *And your handsome face.*

Craig's mind remained a bastion of silence. The longer this continued, the more my concern grew.

Hazel returned to the veranda with a drink in each hand. She handed the eyebright and tonic to me. "A little liquid courage to get you started." *And one for me, for having to endure it.*

I could read everyone's mind except for Craig's. This was not normal.

"How exactly am I supposed to demonstrate my progress with runecraft?" I asked. "Most of the time I practice translating runes in the book and then drawing my own."

My aunt produced her wand. "I'll conjure a rune and you interpret it for us. Simple enough, yes?"

"Easy peasy," I said, shifting uncomfortably.

"I'll start with a basic one." My aunt conjured a rune that looked like a cross between an S and a Z. I was tempted to yell 'Shazam,' mostly because I had a brain block as to the actual answer.

Come on. You know this one, Hazel thought to herself. *The rune for sun.*

"Sun!" I declared triumphantly.

"And what does it mean?" Craig pressed, and I fought the urge to shove my wand up his…

Solace. Success. Hazel's thoughts pushed through my own.

"It can mean solace or success," I said. Silently, I thanked Wren for introducing me to the mind reading spell. Who knew how handy it would be?

Hazel gave me a thumbs up.

"Well try one that's a bit more difficult," Aunt Hyacinth said.

Terrific. Maybe I shouldn't have seemed so confident.

She conjured a rune that I remembered referring to as the X-wing Starfighter in my notes. That was pretty much all I remembered about it.

Day, Ember, Hazel thought. *You can do it.*

It was kind of nice how invested Hazel was in my achievement. Of course, I knew it was mostly because it was a reflection of her, but still. I appreciated her support.

"Day," I said, straightening my shoulders. "And it means hope or happiness." That part spilled from my lips without any help from Hazel. Words like hope and happiness tended to stay with me, probably because I was so desperate to experience them.

Hazel clapped loudly. "Excellent work, Ember."

"I see your time isn't being wasted, Hazel," my aunt said.

"Well done, Ember," Craig said. "And here I thought you were as incompetent as everyone claims. I should have known a Rose couldn't be quite that deficient."

I forced a smile. "Thanks for the vote of confidence, Craig."

My aunt didn't seem the slightest bit bothered by his comment. The witch had stars in her eyes when it came to Craig and that unsettled me more than anything. Hyacinth Rose-Muldoon was generally unflappable, yet this wizard had managed to turn her into a giddy schoolgirl with minimal effort. Something was definitely off with this guy and I was more determined than ever to find out what it was.

CHAPTER FOURTEEN

"Are you certain you're not overreacting?" Alec asked.

I'd listed fifteen different reasons why Craig was probably a secret cave dweller with an axe to grind, but the vampire seemed unimpressed.

We stood at the bar in Elixir, waiting for our drinks. He'd ordered a Breezeburst for me and an old-fashioned for him. The trendy cocktail bar still took my breath away. Bottles of glowing liquid were suspended from the ceiling, attached to the walls, and even built into the flooring. I'd once told Marley it was like standing in the middle of a giant lava lamp. Then she asked me what a lava lamp was and I sulked because I felt old.

"I'm telling you," I insisted. "Craig is bad news and not even of the Bad News Bears variety. He's way worse."

The bartender handed me the bright liquid that resembled red, green, and orange layers of Jell-O. I took a sip of the delightful cocktail and sighed dreamily.

"Do you know this is the first drink you ever bought me?" I asked.

MAGIC & MALADIES

"A Breezeburst?" Alec queried. "What an odd choice."

"You thought I'd like it."

He inclined his head toward the drink in my hand. "Clearly I was right."

"As usual," I said. "You always are, Mr. Smarty Trousers."

His smile faded and he took a soulful sip of his cocktail.

"What's the matter?" I asked. "Did I say something wrong, because where I come from, telling someone they're always right is a compliment?"

"Nothing is wrong," he said.

I wagged a finger. "No, don't do that. You're avoiding confrontation because you're uncomfortable. I can tell because you get that look in your eye."

"And what look is that?"

"The one that tells me you'd rather be elbow-deep in one of your fantasy novels than having this conversation with me right now."

"There's an expression that corresponds to that?"

"Apparently. You've pretty much perfected it. You should offer a YouTube tutorial on it."

He took another long drink and set down his glass. "I worry that you have me on a pedestal," he said. "And I'm even more worried that I can't possibly live up to your version of me."

Whoa. This conversation got real, real fast. "What makes you think that?" I sucked down my cocktail and slid my empty glass across the counter.

"Comments you make. The more you put yourself down, the more you seem to build me up. I don't want you to mistake me for someone I'm not, Ember. I'll only disappoint you."

The bartender wisely had another Breezeburst in my hand before I answered him. "Do I think you're the most amazing living creature on the face of the earth? As a matter of fact, I do, but that doesn't mean I think you're infallible or godlike. I know you're flawed."

"Do you? Because sometimes I wonder."

"Just the other day, your handkerchief in your breast pocket was crooked. Did that change my opinion of you? No siree, it did not."

He couldn't resist a smile. "I'm a vampire, not an angel. Not a werewolf who wears his heart on his sleeve. A relationship with me won't be without its difficulties."

"I spend a lot of time with you, Alec. I've heard you in therapy. I know you have stories to tell." Granted, he was still fairly quiet in our sessions, but I recognized that avoidance was one of his flaws. I didn't pretend he was perfect. "When you're ready, you'll share them with me."

His features softened. "How can you be someone who kicks a tire when you don't feel the pump is filling it with air fast enough, yet you have unending patience when it comes to me?"

"Because, Mr. Fang-tastic. You're super hot and that tire has remnants of roadkill and is in desperate need of rotation."

He chuckled. "I think you should slow down on the cocktails, or at least locate Mr. Andersen before you drink anymore."

"Good plan. See how considerate you are?" I swiveled for a better view of the bar.

"Do you happen to know where we can find Todd Andersen?" Alec asked.

"What do you think I'm...?" I turned to see that he was asking the bartender. "Oh."

The bartender pointed to a booth against the opposite wall where a string bean of an elf sat across from a buxom troll. They held hands across the table and seemed entirely smitten.

"Well, I guess he has a type," I said. Maybe he never got over Shayna's rejection of him and that was the reason he killed her. Only one way to find out.

"Perhaps I should accompany you," Alec said.

I waved him off. "I got this. You stay there on your pedestal with your excellent bird's-eye view of the bar."

He smirked. "I'll keep a bird's-eye on your drink while you're gone."

"No tasting," I called over my shoulder. I sauntered over to Todd's table and suddenly wished I had forgone the cocktail until after the interview.

Neither the elf nor the troll noticed me until I cleared my throat. They were too wrapped up in each other.

"Hi," I said. "Are you Todd Andersen?"

"That's right," the elf said. "Do I know you?"

"I'm Ember Rose and I'm a reporter for *Vox Populi*."

"Oh, yes," he said. "I read it every week."

"You do?" I tried not to sound so shocked. "I mean, you do. That's nice. So I guess you've heard the horrible news about Shayna Masters."

His jaw tensed and he released the troll's hands. "Yeah, I heard."

"Is that the ex you told me about, Todd?" the troll asked. Her voice was much softer than her appearance suggested.

He gave a curt nod. "I saw her recently for the first time in ages. If I'd known it would be the last time…" He couldn't finish the sentence.

"Would you mind if I asked you a few questions?" I asked. "I'm trying to write this article on her and it would be good to get a well-rounded view of her, you know? I don't want to stick to customers of her shop. It's not a complete picture."

"She has a boyfriend. Did you interview him?"

"A little, but he's so shaken up by her death," I said. "I thought I'd try someone with more...distance."

Todd looked at his date. "Would you mind leaving us alone for a couple minutes, Hattie?"

"Sure thing, honey," she said. "I'll go powder my nose." She slid out of the booth.

"Do women still do that?" I asked.

The troll touched her wide green nose. "I'm always shiny. I look like a hormonal dragon when I don't use powder."

"Got it." I took her place across from Todd. "Thanks for speaking with me."

"No problem." He fiddled with the edge of his beverage napkin. "What do you want to know?"

"Let's start with your general impression of her. You were engaged once, so you must've thought pretty highly of her."

Todd grunted. "At the time, sure. She has...Sorry, she had a big personality. Sometimes that was awesome and sometimes that was overwhelming. When we were still hot and heavy, it was awesome."

"What did you find overwhelming about her?"

Todd tipped back his glass of ale and drank. "She could be rude. Said hurtful things. She wasn't trying to be malicious, though, and I knew that. She was just thoughtless sometimes."

"But you overlooked it?"

"Yeah, sure. I was in love with her. You overlook a lot when you're in deep, right?"

"So what changed?" I asked.

"Nothing for me," he said. "She broke off our engagement out of the blue. I was blown away, to be honest. I thought she was the one for me. Not a shred of doubt."

"Were you angry?"

Todd gave a rueful smile. "Who wouldn't be? I felt disposable. I knew she'd broken off an engagement before mine, but I thought…"

"You thought you were different?" I prodded. "Special?"

He rubbed his hand over his cheek. "Yeah. That."

"How long ago was this?"

"A year and a half, I guess."

"And you haven't been in touch since then?" I asked. My head was getting a little fuzzy from the cocktails. Hopefully, I could wrap this up before the alcohol hit me too hard. I'd forgotten how potent those Breezebursts could be.

"Not really," he said. "I sent her a few texts not long after the breakup, wanting answers, but I eventually gave up when she ghosted me. Then I saw her here recently, like I said."

"And how was that?" Running into a former fiancé couldn't be high on the list of happy moments in life.

"Fine for me, but Shayna was…She was in overwhelming mode, let's just say that."

"What do you mean?" I hiccupped and quickly covered my mouth. Apparently, the alcohol was having an effect on multiple body parts.

"She was loud, abrasive, insulted Hattie." He shook his head. "It was a good moment for me, to be honest. I saw her clearly for the first time and realized how truly awful she could be. I got the closure I needed."

"Why do you think she was in overwhelming mode?"

He smirked. "I think she got pissed when she saw that I was happy with Hattie and that we were engaged."

"Oh, congratulations," I said. "That's great." It was good to know that he'd managed to bounce back after heartbreak. I needed to hear those stories, not just for me but for Granger.

"Thanks. I thought Shayna would be happy, too. I figured she didn't want me. What would she care that I was going to marry someone else?"

"But she surprised you?"

He released a breath. "Oh, yeah. She sure did. She seemed annoyed that Hattie's a troll. Felt like I was replacing her, which went against her world view that she was irreplaceable."

I raised my eyebrows. "She said that?"

"In her own way, yeah. She told Hattie that she should try contouring makeup to minimize her features. That Elixir's artificial lights weren't doing her any favors."

After the way Shayna behaved at the wedding, this information didn't really surprise me. "Was Hattie upset?"

"Actually, no." Todd appeared pleased. "Rolled right off those sturdy shoulders of hers. She could tell that Shayna was lashing out."

I frowned, remembering what Lois had told me. "So you and Shayna didn't have a disagreement or anything that night?"

"No," Todd said. "Shayna was clearly shaken up and went back to her boyfriend or whoever he is."

"Franco was with her?" I asked. I downed the rest of my drink. It was too tasty to let sit for long. Probably not the best idea when I was interviewing a suspect, but he didn't *know* he was a suspect, so really I was providing a cover.

"They came in together, but she left him in a booth when she came over to talk to me," Todd said. "I think she expected me to react differently to seeing her and, of course, she didn't know about Hattie until that moment."

So it seemed that the reason Shayna had been upset when she shared the story with Lois was because Todd was engaged, not because he'd said or done something horrible to her. Interesting.

"Tyra was also here that night," Todd continued. "I don't know if they chose to avoid or snap at each other, but they were definitely in the bar at the same time."

"Who's Tyra?" And why did that name sound familiar?

"Tyra Langley, one of Shayna's regular customers." He paused. "Well, she was back when Shayna and I were together. They had a falling out from what I've heard."

"Do you know why?" I asked.

He shrugged. "Business. Money. It was Shayna's primary focus, so if there was an issue, that was generally the reason. Tyra's a wardrobe designer so she's always in the market for the kinds of items at Be-switched."

A gear in my brain clicked. Tyra Langley had attended the wedding. Shayna had made a caustic remark about her. I hadn't registered it at the time because—let's face it—Shayna made caustic remarks about everyone.

"Thanks. That's helpful, Todd." Very helpful.

Out of the corner of my eye, I noticed Hattie lingering. I turned and waved her over. "Thanks for your help, Todd, and good luck to you both." I vacated the booth so that Hattie could reclaim her seat.

Todd held up a finger. "Would you mind not printing anything bad about Shayna, at least anything I disclosed? I mean, she's dead now. No point in dancing on her grave, right? I loved her once. I'd like to respect that."

Hattie reached across the table and squeezed his hand. "We should send flowers or something to her boyfriend."

"That's a good idea," Todd said. "I'll do it first thing in the morning."

As soon as I stood to leave the booth, the alcohol hit me. Hard. Unfortunately, that was the moment I ran smack into Deputy Bolan. Well, his tiny leprechaun head ran smack into the soft part of my belly. At least there was a cushion.

"This place is disorienting," I grumbled, struggling to maintain my balance. Who thought it was a good idea to have all these colors blinding a bunch of inebriated customers? "I need to speak with the interior designer. Stat."

"What you need is to stop swaying long enough to have a drink of water."

"What we need is to get Granger back on the straight and narrow before it's too late. His career depends on us." I patted the leprechaun on the head. "Has anyone ever told you that you're both menacing and adorable at the same time? That's no easy feat."

He glowered. "Can we avoid the phrase 'straight and narrow?'"

"What's wrong with that?"

"One, because it's a path you can't even walk right now. Two, because it implies that straight and narrow is the good path and that anything not straight and not narrow is bad."

I squinted at him. "Is this a gay leprechaun thing?"

He exhaled and rubbed the bridge of his nose. "How many drinks have you had, Rose?"

I pressed my nose against the empty glass. "This one was about ten sips. I finished it while I was interviewing our suspect." I gesticulated to Todd in the booth behind us.

Deputy Bolan groaned. "You can't conduct official business while intoxicated, Rose."

"Why not? You do it while being short and green. How can anyone take you seriously?" I tweaked his ear. "I mean, look at that adorable face. It's like being interrogated by a glow-in-the-dark puppy."

"Where's your babysitter?" he growled.

"You mean Alec?" I scanned the crowded bar. "He's the *hottest* babysitter, isn't he? I would love to sit on his lap all night long, if you know what I mean."

"It's impossible to misinterpret any of your sentences," the deputy replied. "That's what happens when you avoid complex grammar."

I laughed and then burped loudly. Deputy Bolan rolled

his beady eyes and took me by the elbow. "Come on, Detective Rose. Let's get you back to your headquarters."

"So I'll be safe?"

"No, so the rest of us will."

CHAPTER FIFTEEN

I DECIDED to pay a visit to the one woman with insight into Granger aside from me. I hadn't seen Mrs. Nash since I ended my relationship with the sheriff. The cowardly part of me wanted to turn and run the other way, but all of me cared too much for the werewolf to let fear take hold. I owed it to him to help get him back on track.

As I parked the car, I caught sight of her along the side of the modest house, knee-deep in gardening. My stomach fluttered as I forged ahead.

"Hi, Mrs. Nash," I said. I sounded more hesitant than I intended, my nerves leading the way on this one.

She gazed up at me with a friendly smile and shielded her eyes from the intense sunlight. "Well, isn't this a wonderful surprise?" She clambered to her feet and dusted off her knees. "Are you thirsty? There's fresh lemon fizz in the fridge."

"I have a policy of never turning down a glass of homemade lemon fizz," I said.

She walked around the corner and entered the house

through the screen door. She peeled off her gardening gloves and tossed them into a bucket on the floor next to the kitchen counter. "I'm going to go out on a limb and assume that you're here to talk about my son." She didn't look at me. Instead, she busied herself in the kitchen, pulling two glasses from the cabinet. Each one was etched with a design of a pineapple.

"Yes, but which one?" I asked. "These days, it's pretty difficult to tell them apart."

She crossed the room to take the pitcher of lemon fizz out of the fridge. "You've noticed, have you?"

I settled on a stool at the counter. "Who hasn't? It seems to be a main topic of conversation in Starry Hollow right now."

Her brow creased. "That's unfortunate. I gather that's why you're here. You want to see if I can talk to him?"

"Well, there is that, but there's also the broader question of why? What's gotten into him?"

She poured a glass and slid it across the counter to me. "I think we both know why, Ember. We don't need to be the sheriff to figure that one out."

My face grew flushed. Of course his mother knew. They were very close and I had no doubt he'd confided in her to some degree. That was definitely an area where Granger surpassed Alec. The werewolf wasn't afraid to express his emotions to those he cared about. At least, that was the Granger I knew. This look-alike Granger was someone else entirely.

"Have you seen him recently?" I asked. I brought the glass to my lips and let the bubbles tickle my nose. Lemon fizz was one of those beverages that had no equal in the human world. Describing it as carbonated lemonade didn't do it justice. There seemed to be a magical quality to it.

"Yes, both boys were here on Sunday for dinner."

"You're living the dream," I said. "What mom doesn't want her grown sons coming by for Sunday dinners?"

She gave me a pointed look. "Your aunt seems to do quite well in that regard."

That was certainly true. Aunt Hyacinth's Sunday dinners at Thornhold were a staple in our lives. How she managed to command everyone's presence on a weekly basis was an impressive feat, especially with the family's busy schedules. Sterling was the only one who occasionally skipped, but Hyacinth didn't seem to mind. I knew she would mind a hell of a lot more if Florian was the one who opted to dine elsewhere.

"How did he seem at dinner?" I asked.

She took a long drink and set down her glass. "I'll say this much. It's been nice to see my boys getting along so well lately. In fact, I haven't seen them get on like this since they were young."

"Presumably, this is because Granger is more in tune with Wyatt these days."

She chuckled. "That's a nice way of putting it. Then again, you're a journalist. I guess you have a natural way with words."

Now it was my turn to laugh. "I don't have a natural way with anything. I'm only a journalist because my aunt decided it was the best job for me in Starry Hollow." Not that I objected. I'd come to enjoy my job. I felt like more of a role model for Marley working as a reporter than I did as a repo agent. I mean, I put a roof over our heads and scraped by with that job so I was proud of myself for that, but it wasn't the life I'd imagined for myself. Not that Starry Hollow was either. Who could have imagined being transported to a magical town?

"I'm his mother, so I'm only getting a glimpse of what's going on," Mrs. Nash said. "Doesn't stop me from getting reports from others, though. Plenty of pack members have called or texted with a recent Granger sighting, usually at their local watering hole."

"And hitting on one of their daughters?"

She pressed her lips together, seemingly unwilling to speak ill of her son. "I know you care about him, Ember, and I imagine that's the reason you're here."

"There's a chance he might lose his job if this behavior continues," I said. "You didn't hear that from me. Deputy Bolan and I are trying to crack his current case so that he isn't fired."

She sucked in her cheeks. "I didn't realize he was slacking off at work. I only thought he was annoying paranormals with his newfound libido." She stared intently at the lemon fizz in her glass. "I think this is his way of trying to move on from you. He's taken on this persona."

"You mean Wyatt's persona," I said.

"It was hard when their father died," she said. "I knew I wasn't a perfect mom, but I seemed to do okay with Granger. I've always thought Wyatt would be Wyatt no matter what our circumstances had been. Who knows?"

"You've done a wonderful job with Granger," I said. "Whatever's going on with him now, I'm sure it's only temporary. We just need to find a way to snap him out of it."

She met my gaze. "Seems ironic. It was only a few weeks ago when he was here and I was encouraging him to move on from you. He said it would be easier if he could just forget you, but I told him that he didn't really want that. My heart broke into a million pieces when their father died but never once did I want to forget him. When you love someone, you end up carrying a piece of them with you wherever you go. You're always better off for having loved someone. Forgetting… That's disrespectful to both parties."

It was difficult to listen to his mother talk about our relationship, to talk about the aftermath. I knew I had hurt him and I would always regret that. He deserved better than what I could give him.

"I tried to talk to him," I said. "It just felt more like I was talking to a stranger. Not that he'd forgotten me, more like he'd forgotten himself."

"Maybe I'll have a chat with him when Wyatt isn't around to influence him," she said. "He'd be devastated to lose his job. Being the sheriff is his life. He's had a hard enough time coming back from you. I don't know that he could come back from that, too."

I swilled my lemon fizz, not wanting to waste a single drop. "Your homemade is the best, seriously."

"I'd be happy to send some home with you," she said. "Share some with that sweet daughter of yours."

I was sorely tempted, but I didn't feel right about taking anything from Granger's mom. I didn't want this visit to be self-serving in any way. "Keep it for Granger. Pour him a glass when you have your talk. And please let me know how it goes. Deputy Bolan and I will be working hard to close this case, but inevitably there will be a case after that. The problem isn't going to go away until his behavior does."

She moved closer and hugged me. I'd forgotten how affectionate his family was. "I appreciate you coming, Ember. I'm sure it wasn't easy."

"I would do anything for him," I said. Well, that wasn't strictly true. Otherwise, we'd still be together.

Mrs. Nash squeezed me hard. "I've already lost my husband. I don't want to lose my son, too. Not to heartache. Not to anything."

"I'll see what I can do," I said softly.

. . .

Magnus Destry lived in a concrete house that would have looked more at home in California than Starry Hollow. It was perched on a cliff overlooking the ocean and I was immediately filled with view envy. I noticed a landing strip for broomsticks that ran alongside the driveway. Clever.

I knocked on the door and waited. According to Florian, Magnus was somewhat of a homebody. Luckily, my cousin had been too focused on his dart game to ask me any follow-up questions.

The door clicked open and Magnus stood in the doorway wearing a long, black cloak, jeans, and black slippers. Beneath his cloak, I glimpsed a red T-shirt.

"Hey, Magnus. I hope you don't mind me stopping by. I could really use your help with something."

The High Priest stared at me blankly for a moment as though trying to remember my name. "Now isn't a good time. Why don't you come back sometime between yesterday and never?" He began to close the door, but I stuck out my foot to prevent it from shutting.

"I promise I won't take up too much of your time," I said. "It's just that I'm doing research on an ancestor and I keep hitting a brick wall. Someone suggested you'd be the right guy to ask."

Magnus sniffed. "Well, I don't see why your aunt can't help you in that case. We all know how committed she is to her heritage."

"I don't want her to know," I said simply.

That got his attention. Slowly, he opened the door further. "I beg your pardon? You want to keep this little research project away from your aunt's all-seeing eyes?"

"That's right. It can be our little secret."

A smile emerged and he stepped aside. "Do come in, Ember. Don't mind the mess."

I stepped into the Spartan foyer. There were clean lines as

far as the eye could see. "You and I have different ideas about what constitutes a mess. You could have amazing parties here and *make* a mess. Why don't you entertain more often?"

"I'm an INTJ. I find socializing exhausting," he said. "The monthly coven meetings are enough social interaction for me."

"High Priest is an interesting choice for the most introverted of introverts."

"It isn't a choice," he said darkly. "It's a calling." He guided me to a sectional sofa made of black leather. As he sat, his cloak fell open and revealed more of the red T-shirt underneath.

"Sweet baby Harry Potter," I exclaimed. "That's a Platform 9 3/4 T-shirt. Where did you get that?"

Magnus quickly drew the sides of his cloak back across the shirt. "I don't know what you mean."

I stared at him, incredulous. "Yes, you do. That's a Harry Potter reference. Magnus, are you a closet Potterhead?"

He seemed to waver. "Do you promise not to tell anyone?"

I barked a laugh. "Who am I going to tell? The only one who knows Harry Potter around here is Marley."

Excitement sparked in his dark eyes. "I used my passport to take a trip to the human world last month and it was life-changing. I watched all the films, bought the complete set of hardcovers, and came back with more souvenirs than I could carry. I had to have a bottomless bag expedited to me for the trip home."

"Sounds like you had a good time."

He tore off his cloak and adjusted the hem of his T-shirt proudly. "Which house are you?" He peered at me. "Please don't say Hufflepuff or I don't think I'll be able to help you."

I admonished him with a pointer finger. "Listen, you've

been a fan for five minutes compared with the rest of the world. Don't go beating on Hufflepuffs."

He shrugged. "I'm a Slytherclaw. It's in my nature, apparently."

"Marley is a Ravendor and I'm a Gryffinpuff."

He scrutinized me. "Gryffinpuff? Are you sure about that?"

"Of course. Why wouldn't I be?" And I only took the test three times to get that result. "Can we get down to business? I don't want to keep you from salivating over the Pottermore website."

"Why don't we discuss this downstairs? Then I can show you the treasures from my trip. I keep them out of sight because I know that no one else will understand or appreciate them." He paused. "And I detest mess, at least in the main living space."

I lifted my bag back over my shoulder. "Lead on, Mr. Slytherclaw."

I followed Magnus to an open doorway and down a flight of stairs. We emptied into an open-plan space that spanned the entire lower-level. The front of the room was made of glass to maximize the exterior view of the water. The interior view—well, it looked like Hogwarts had exploded. There were banners of the four houses on the walls and retro-style pictures of Hogsmeade, Hogwarts, and Diagon Alley. On a long table in the middle of the room was a replica of Hogwarts made out of Lego. Figurines were scattered across the table in various scenes. The centaur Firenze. Hagrid. Harry and Buckbeak, the hippogriff. Magnus clearly had spent a lot of time and thought putting this together. Or he'd simply used magic. Either way, it was a Harry Potter wonderland.

"Isn't it amazing?" he asked.

"Wow," I said. "I'll be honest. This was not at all what I was expecting."

"I'm a grown wizard and I've never connected with material like this before," he said. "I mean, I've always been an avid reader and have enjoyed characters and world-building in other stories, but something about this one really grabbed me by the shoulders and shook me hard."

"I can see that," I said. Marley would have a field day down here. "None of it bothers you for its inaccuracies?"

"With such a compelling story, who cares? Besides, theirs is a different system entirely. It's fun to explore other wizarding worlds."

"Speaking of exploring…" I set my bag on the table and he lurched forward.

"No, no. Please don't put anything too close to Hogwarts. Use that table over there." He pointed to a smaller table against the northern wall that he hadn't managed to cover in memorabilia yet.

I crossed the room and emptied the bag onto the table. Magnus joined me, his brow lifting when he noticed the ancient grimoire.

"I tend to only see books like that in the archives," he commented.

I frowned. "What archives? At the library?"

"No. The official coven archives, of course," he said. He motioned to the book. "May I?"

"That's why I'm here."

Magnus carefully turned each page of the grimoire. "It's a beauty. I love the smell of these old books. Where did you find this one?"

"My aunt gave this grimoire and the wand to my daughter for her birthday," I said. "This Book of Shadows I found recently."

Magnus shifted away from the grimoire to pick up the

Book of Shadows. He pressed the cover to his nose and inhaled deeply. "Buried treasure," he murmured.

"Pretty much," I said.

"I gather these belonged to a Rose," he said.

"Her name was Ivy. She was a High Priestess."

His expression darkened. "Yes, the scandalous one. I recall the story. There's a section devoted to her in the archives."

My pulse began to race. "There's an entire section about Ivy Rose in the archives? How do I access them?"

"You can't," he said simply. "Only High Priestesses and High Priests can view the archives."

"Can you tell me what you remember reading about her? All I know is that she had to step down as High Priestess and was stripped of her magic for use of excessive force."

"Ivy Rose was one of the most powerful witches in our coven's history," he said. "Too powerful, even for herself. It was said that she had inherited the most gifts from your common ancestor."

"The One True Witch?" I queried.

He ran his thumb along the carvings of the wand. "That's the one. I've been a general believer that the magic of the ancient witch has been diluted over the centuries to become meaningless, but Ivy is one of those cases that gives me pause."

"Is that why you resent my aunt? You think she overplays her abilities?"

He faced me. "Who said that?"

"Someone observant," I said. "They weren't trying to start trouble. They were only trying to help me find someone willing to help me without ratting me out to my aunt."

"There is so much concentrated power here," he said. "You can feel it, can't you?"

"Can't stop feeling it. The wand in particular seems to have a lot of negative energy attached to it," I said. "We've tried cleansing it, but the power seems locked in, if that makes sense. Marley's been using it, but something about it just doesn't feel right. Almost as though it's holding back."

Magnus brought the wand to his nostrils and smelled it. "I see what you mean."

"Are you some sort of secret wizard-shifter hybrid? What's with the olfactory obsession?"

"We all have our magical strengths and weaknesses," he said. "I have developed an acute sense of smell, mainly to detect magic."

"Before you even think about shoving the wand up your nose, tell me what you know about Ivy and her use of excessive force," I said. "Did she hurt someone? Was she evil?"

"No, she was most definitely not evil. She was an excellent witch and a devoted High Priestess. She simply didn't have the training that would have aided her in honing her skills. She had more power than she could handle and no one equipped to mentor her. She needed someone at least as strong as she was, but that individual wizard didn't exist, sadly."

"What about her upbringing? She attended the Black Cloak Academy. She became High Priestess. I don't think they hand that title out willy-nilly."

"No, they most certainly do not." He turned his attention to the Book of Shadows and attempted to open it. The cover didn't budge. "Merciful Hecate. I can't open it."

"Nope. Seems to be warded shut."

He gaped at me. "And your aunt had this in her possession but was unable to undo the spell?"

"Not this one," I admitted. "I found this one buried in the garden. I haven't mentioned it to her."

Magnus gave me an appraising look. "Have I mentioned you're really growing on me?"

"Let me say this—I don't enjoy going behind her back.

Mostly because I don't want to incur her wrath, but also because she's been unfailingly kind and generous to us. I hate to feel this way, but I do and I can't ignore it."

Magnus produced his wand. "A bit of recon, if you don't mind." He uttered an incantation as he dragged the tip of his wand around the edges of the book. "Fascinating."

"You can't open it?"

"I don't even want to try until we know more. It could be booby-trapped." He tucked away his wand. "You think her Book of Shadows has helpful information in connection with the wand?"

"It's her most personal possession," I said. "Whatever isn't in those archives will be in here. I guarantee it."

"And somewhere between their story and her story will lie the truth." Magnus inhaled sharply. "I would be willing to take a look in the archives for you. I admit, the petty part of me finds a fallen Rose a worthy subject of study."

I nearly threw myself at his slipper-clad feet. "Would you? That would be so amazing."

Magnus squinted at me. "Why is this so important to you? More importantly, why is it a secret?"

"Mainly, I want to be sure that Ivy's personal effects aren't going to cause any harm to my daughter," I explained. "My aunt is all about family, yet she's kept Ivy's wand and grimoire in her possession for years. Instead of handing them down to one of her own children, she gave them to mine, which she didn't even know existed until the last year. I just…don't trust it."

"Understood. I'll nose around the archives and let you know what I find." He rubbed his hands together. "I'll be like an auror for the Ministry of Magic."

"Thank you so much, Magnus. I really appreciate it." I started for the staircase, but he moved to block my path.

"I'll do it on one condition."

Ugh, terrific. I knew there had to be a catch. "What's that?"

"You help me put together this Lego set with Ron and the giant spider. I'm having terrible trouble with the legs and I want to resist using magic. It's more fun to do it the human way."

Personally, I found it more frustrating than fun, but I wasn't about to turn him down given what he was willing to do for me. "My fine motor skills aren't the best, but I'll give it a try." The mention of the word 'try' automatically triggered Yoda's voice in my head. "Do or do not. There is no try," I mimicked under my breath.

Magnus's gaze flicked to me. "What's that a reference to?"

"Nothing," I said quickly. "I made it up." The last thing this wizard needed was an introduction to Star Wars. Next thing I knew there'd be a full-scale Millennium Falcon in here.

Magnus handed me a box filled with tiny pieces. "Let's have a bit of fun, shall we?"

CHAPTER SIXTEEN

I STOOD on Tyra Langley's doorstep and searched for the bell. Although I didn't find one, I noticed an indentation in the shape of a head in front of me on the door. I realized that I was probably meant to place my face in there for recognition. It seemed more science fiction than magical, but I decided to give it a whirl. I stood on my toes and rested my chin on the narrow ledge and waited. I wasn't sure how she handled shorter visitors like dwarfs and leprechauns. This method suggested an extreme prejudice. A moment later, a disembodied voice emanated from the other side of the door.

"I don't know you," the voice snapped.

"No, my name is Ember. I'm writing a story about Shayna Masters and was wondering if you could answer a few questions." It was slightly awkward to talk with my head somewhat on a platter.

"Why would any publication worth its salt write an article about that beast?"

"Shayna was a member of this community," I said. "She was a successful business owner and she was brutally murdered at a local wedding. That warrants coverage in my view."

"Whatever," she muttered.

I returned my head to its normal position. "Do you think I might be able to come in so that we can discuss this in a more civilized fashion?"

I heard a small groan. "Fine, but you have to take off your shoes and use my special anti-germ tonic on your hands."

"Sounds reasonable," I said. Reasonably neurotic.

The door cracked open and I slipped inside. The first thing I noticed was that the interior of the house was bathed in light pink. It was like walking inside a ballet slipper. Even Tyra wore a flowing pink dress with spaghetti straps. Each finger sported at least one ring—all rose gold. When I looked down to take off my shoes, I saw that even her toes wore rings.

"Here's the tonic." She spritzed my hands with clear liquid from a bottle that she kept on a table in the entryway. The shoes went into a tray underneath the table. It reminded me of airport security.

Tyra walked into an adjoining room, the hem of her dress swishing around her ankles.

"I understand you were one of Shayna's regular customers," I began.

"Not anymore," Tyra said. "And not just because she's dead either. I told her I would never set foot back in her shop again and I meant it."

"Would you mind telling me what happened?"

"She tried to cheat me, that's what happened. Nobody cheats Tyra Langley. I'm one of the most respected wardrobe designers in the nation."

"How did she try to cheat you?" I set my purse on the cushion next to me and noticed Tyra flinch.

"Would you mind ever so much keeping your purse on your lap?" she asked.

I cast a quick glance at my purse. "Is there a problem?"

"Well, you know how purses are. You bring them to a restaurant. You set them down on the dirty floor at your table where food has fallen and shoes have crossed over a hundred times." She scrunched her nose in disgust.

"And you're worried about the bottom of my purse leaving germs on your sofa cushion?"

She offered a relieved smile. "Exactly. I'm so glad you get it."

Sheesh. King Arthur himself couldn't pull that stick out of her butt. I dutifully moved the bag so that it was no longer besmirching her pristine cushion. "I'm surprised someone with your exacting standards would be willing to shop in a place like Be-switched. All those items are secondhand."

"Oh, I know, but Shayna had every item cleaned the moment she acquired it. I trusted her. She maintained a wonderfully diverse inventory filled with high quality items. That troll definitely had an eye, I'll give her that."

"So what changed?"

She slotted her fingers together and rested them on her knee. "I was sourcing a wardrobe for a pilot episode of a television show and I knew that Shayna had some vintage clothing that would be perfect."

"How did she try to cheat you? She tried to overcharge you because she knew you really wanted them?"

Tyra's expression soured. "No, worse than that. I honestly don't know what possessed her to do it. She had to know that I would figure it out." She drew a delicate breath. "Two of the dresses she claimed were vintage were actually from Bull's-eye."

"The chain store?"

"Yes. Can you believe the audacity of that woman?"

"Are you sure she knew that they weren't authentic?"

"Oh, she knew. From what I gather, she'd heard about the project in advance and went and found dresses that she knew would seem appropriate. Apparently, she didn't have anything in stock and didn't want to lose my business to anyone else. Shayna could be fiercely competitive."

"And what happened when you found out?"

"Well, I went to confront her, of course. I couldn't let her get away with that. I marched right down to Be-switched and demanded a refund."

"And did she give you one?" I had noticed the no refund policy on a sign in the shop.

"She refused. I was outraged. She knew perfectly well that she'd tried to fool me, and even in the face of that, she wouldn't admit any wrongdoing or refund my money."

"That must've made you very angry," I said.

"You're not kidding," Tyra said. "I warned her that I would drag her reputation through the mud and that she would regret ever trying to take advantage of me. I mean, my entire reputation depends upon making the right choices. If I had produced those dresses for the show and someone had discovered the truth before me, my career would be over."

Sounded like a pretty strong motive for murder to me.

"I understand you attended the wedding where Shayna was murdered."

She flinched. "Yes, I was there. And I requested a seat far away from Shayna so that we could avoid each other and spare everyone the discomfort."

"Did you have any interaction at all with her at the wedding or the reception?"

"Not a word. Not even a glance in her direction. You can ask my date. I didn't even bother to stay for the rest of the reception after my first drink because I didn't want to have to deal with her. Plus, I couldn't abide a reception on the beach." She shuddered. "All that sand everywhere. Nightmare."

"Do you recall how long you stayed at the reception?"

"Not even half an hour," Tyra said. "My date and I went out for a lovely meal afterward at Maison Magique. If you haven't been there, I highly recommend it. It's superb and I know the owner keeps a very clean kitchen."

"Thanks for the tip." Her alibi would be easy enough to check out.

Tyra unclasped her hands. "I'm sorry she's dead, of course, and I hope they catch whoever's responsible. I'm not a monster."

"Of course not."

"I'm sure she rubbed the wrong paranormal the wrong way. It was bound to happen eventually, given Shayna's robust personality. Personally, I wouldn't have dared get close enough to be able to murder her. Just breathing the same air as that vile creature made me reach for my inhaler."

And with Tyra's germ anxiety, it was unlikely that she'd have ventured within spitting distance of the portable toilets.

My phone buzzed in my purse. "Excuse me. I always have to check in case it's my daughter."

"Oh, you have a child." She seemed doubly relieved that she'd hosed me down with tonic.

The text was from Linnea. *Need you. Urgent.*

That didn't bode well. Nothing was ever urgent with Linnea.

"Thanks for your time," I said quickly. "I need to go now." I sprang to my feet and hustled toward the door.

"Don't forget your shoes!" Tyra called.

The moment I stepped outside, I called Linnea. "What's wrong?"

"Are you busy?" Linnea sounded like she was whispering.

"Who cares? You said it's urgent. Are you okay?"

"I'm fine, but would you mind coming down to The Arched Cat?"

"The yoga studio on Thistle Street?"

"That's right," she said. "I'm here for class with Iris Sandstone and Granger is here acting like a dog in heat. I don't even understand why he's at a yoga class. He's wearing denim for goddess's sake. There's no flexibility in that material."

Yes, because that was the most alarming issue right now. "I'll be there as fast as I can." I clicked off the phone and raced to my car.

I didn't want everyone to know about Granger. Of course, he wasn't doing himself any favors by acting out in public. The Arched Cat would be full of coven members. Word was bound to get back to Aunt Hyacinth, which meant that the Council of Elders would be informed. Iris Sandstone was the High Priestess of the coven. How foolish could he be? Then again, Granger had always had a bee in his bonnet about my aunt and our family. He resented her unofficial authority in town. He felt that my family was paid too much deference simply because of our name, not that I disagreed. Personally, being a descendent of the One True Witch didn't change my perception of myself, it only changed others' perceptions of me. Briefly, I wondered whether Ivy had experienced any backlash as a powerful Rose. Maybe it made her unpopular or put her at odds with coven members who weren't from a prominent family. In Ivy's day, the only type of celebrities in the world would have been paranormals like the One True Witch. It would have been an impossible burden to bear.

I parked as close as I could and ran the couple of blocks to the yoga studio. The yogis were in the process of unrolling their mats as I entered. I spotted Granger flexing for one of the witches in front of the mirror. While she seemed amused, the High Priestess did not. Iris watched from the front of the studio, a dangerous glint in her eye. I decided to deal with her first so that I could give Granger my full attention.

"Ember, I didn't expect to see you here. You're more than welcome to borrow a mat, but you might want to change first."

I glanced down at my clothes. "I'm not here for yoga," I said quickly. "I can see that Sheriff Nash is making a nuisance of himself. Maybe consider me your saving grace?"

Her gaze darted from the sheriff and back to me. "At first I thought Wyatt was here to harass Linnea. Imagine my surprise when I realized it was the sheriff."

"He's not himself right now, but he will be. I promise."

Iris regarded me silently, seeming to understand that I was asking for discretion. Finally, she said, "Very well then. If you manage to extract him now, I'll say no more about it."

I clasped my hands together in a gesture of appreciation. "Thank you so much, Iris. You're the best."

Linnea mouthed a silent thank you as I maneuvered myself next to Granger and looped my arm through his. "So sorry to interrupt, but I need the sheriff for a very important matter. It's about the murder he's going to solve all by himself." I didn't wait for a response from either one of them. I simply dragged the werewolf into an empty corridor. Before I could detach from him, he snaked an arm around my waist and pressed me against the wall.

"This was your plan all along, was it?" he murmured. "To get me alone?"

I pushed my hands against his chest to put distance between us. "No, Sheriff. If I'd wanted that, there are a thousand other places I could have tracked you down. I need you to check yourself before you wreck yourself." I squeezed my eyes closed. "Okay, nobody says that anymore, but I still need you to do that. Your behavior is out of control."

"Then try to keep up," he said. Without warning, he pressed his lips to mine. I was so shocked that I acted on instinct, grabbing him by the earlobe and pulling. Hard.

"So that's a no?" he said, wincing.

"Granger Nash, stop it this instant. Are you trying to get yourself killed?"

"No, I'm trying to get myself kissed by the prettiest witch in town." He cocked his head, looking at me. "Surprisingly, she doesn't seem interested."

"Granger, you know I'm with Alec now. You need to calm down these wolf hormones of yours. You have gone full Wyatt and nobody is amused." Except maybe Wyatt.

"What's the big deal?" he asked. "My personal life is my business. If you and I want to explore our inner animal in the hallway, nobody has to know." He lowered his hand to the small of my back and I smacked it away.

"This isn't you!"

"Sure it is," he said. "Sheriff Granger Nash. Says so right here on my star." He tapped the shiny piece of metal affixed to his shirt.

"No, that's your name and your title, but this…" I circled a finger in front of his face. "This is not who you are."

He took a step backward and lowered his gaze. "That's the problem," he said. "I don't seem to know who I am anymore. I keep trying to figure it out, to see what feels right, but nothing works. I figured following my brother's lead was my best bet."

My jaw unhinged. "Are you on some form of magical crack? Why would you ever think Wyatt was a role model in any way, shape, or form? You know better."

He frowned, appearing to be confused. "I don't think I do."

"Granger, I've seen you do things recently that I can never forget unless I…" I stopped abruptly as my memories rewound to Haverford House, when I'd joked to myself about taking a potion to forget what I knew about Artemis and Jefferson's unusual relationship.

"Unless you what?" Granger prodded.

"Forget," I murmured. "You wanted to forget. That's what you told your mother."

"You spoke to her?"

Synapses were sparking all over my brain. "Great popcorn balls of fire. You did this to yourself, Granger. You took something."

He looked at me blankly. "What did I take?"

I gripped him by the arms. "Take me back to your place."

He shot me a look of amusement. "Now you want to come back to my place? I thought you said you were with Alec. Make up your mind."

I smacked his arm. "Not for that. I'm trying to help you, you shaggy mutt. Now take me back to your place before I change my mind and leave you twisting in the wind."

"Your wish is my command, pretty witch." He motioned for me to go first.

It was only when we reached the street that I realized he hadn't driven his car. "You're riding a motorcycle?"

"You like it? Seems to get a lot of attention from the ladies."

I shook my head. "Just get on."

He climbed on the bike and he wasn't wrong. He did look damn sexy on it. "I need a helmet," I said.

"Spoilsport," he said, and handed me one. Reckless Granger didn't wear one, but I bit my tongue.

I climbed on behind him and wrapped my arms around his waist. It was a quick ride to his place. I tried not to hold him too tightly or lean too closely. I didn't want to send the wrong signals. I only wanted to help him.

Once inside, I began rifling through cupboards and drawers, looking for anything that he might've taken. A potion. A note with a spell. Anything that might explain his warped behavior.

He sidled up to me as I opened his bathroom cabinet. "I think what you're looking for is in the drawer in my bedside table," he said suggestively.

I elbowed him in the stomach. "Down, wolf. I told you that's not what this is about." I whipped around to face him. "The truth is that you took something to forget me. Only it didn't work. Whatever you took, it seems to have made you forget *you* instead."

His expression shifted to something between a frown and a smile. "Why would I want to forget you?"

I glanced upward, struggling to find a way of easing the pain. "I hurt you, badly. I think you might have gone in search of a spell or a potion that would make you forget that you cared for me. Whatever you did, you haven't forgotten me, but you have forgotten you." I jabbed a finger into his chest where his heart was. "You seem to have forgotten the very essence of who you are—at your core. Instead, you've teased out too much wolf. We need to get the real Granger back."

He grabbed my hand and kissed my finger. "You're Ember Rose. I could never forget you."

Gently, I tugged my hand away. We had to stay focused. "No matter which version of Granger is here right now, your habits are probably much the same. If you were going to take a potion, where would you keep it?"

He stroked the stubble on his rugged jawline. "Probably on the second shelf in the cabinet next to my fridge. That's where I keep vitamins and anything I have to take."

I didn't hesitate. I zipped into the kitchen and opened the cabinet door. Sure enough, I saw a bottle with bright orange liquid inside. Only half the contents remained. It reminded me of the penicillin I used to take as a child whenever I had strep throat. I snatched the bottle from the cabinet for a closer look. The label read Forget-Me-Yes. I squeezed the bottle in my hand.

"This is it, Granger. This is what you took." I scanned the label for more information. I needed to go to the potion maker at Charmed, I'm Sure and find out how to reverse the effects.

He tucked a stray hair behind my ear. Desire burned in his deep brown eyes. "Are you sure you don't want to stay for a little while? Nobody has to know."

I gave him a long, lingering look. "We would know, Granger. We would know."

CHAPTER SEVENTEEN

I'D LEFT my car at The Arched Cat, so I had to get to Potions Lane on foot. I ran through the heart of town as fast as I could. I passed the Painted Pixies and Silver Moon headquarters. The Muse fountain and Shooting Star. I slowed as I neared Charmed, I'm Sure. As much as I wanted to update Deputy Bolan with my discovery, I didn't want to waste a moment. I needed to get the antidote to this potion and administer it to the sheriff. He'd be horrified to realize that he'd shirked his responsibilities, especially given Shayna's murder. While he was busy playing fast and loose with every woman within reach, someone was literally getting away with murder.

I entered the shop and made a beeline for the counter. I didn't recognize this salesclerk. He was a short wizard with a T-shirt that read *Fun Run to Mordor* and a picture of Mount Doom from *Lord of the Rings* in the background. Well, at least we were dealing with a fan of the human world—or the human world's interpretation of the fantasy world. He and Magnus had more in common than they probably knew.

I slapped my hands on the counter. "I need your help."

The wizard smiled. "That's cool. You're that Rose chick, right? The one from New York?"

"New Jersey. I'm Ember."

"I'm Rafe. I'm in your coven. I've seen you at meetings, but I always sit in the back and you're always up in the front with your family."

"Nice to meet you, Rafe. I have a situation and I could really use your help." I pulled the potion bottle from my pocket and set it on the counter. "Did you sell this to Sheriff Nash?"

He picked up the bottle and studied the label. "Nah, dawg. Wasn't me. The ID number here in the corner tells you which one of us made it. 66 is Declan."

"Is Declan around?"

Rafe sat on his stool and spun around. "Nope. Went on holiday to Mistfall. He's been saving for like a year. Can you imagine saving for a year to go somewhere?"

Right now, I was imagining throttling Rafe's neck. "Okay, listen. What do you know about this potion? I need it to be reversed immediately. Whatever you have to do to make that happen, do it."

Rafe's eyes practically bugged out of his head. "Lady Rose, man. This is way above my pay grade. I make the basic potions. I wouldn't know how to handle this one."

"Somebody has to," I insisted. "Who else can we ask? Call Declan in Mistfall if you have to. This is urgent. If I don't get satisfaction, you're going to bring the wrath of the entire Rose family down upon the shop." Rarely did I invoke the Rose name, but this seemed like the appropriate occasion.

Rafe tipped backwards and nearly fell off the stool. He managed to catch himself by throwing a hand against the wall. "Chill, Lady Rose. No wrath required. I'm going to sort you out."

"I'm not the one who needs sorting," I said sharply.

"Sheriff Nash is. This stupid potion has made him forget who he is."

Rafe looked intrigued. "Like he forgets he's the sheriff? Who does he think he is?"

I didn't feel like getting into detail. "Basically, he thinks he's his brother, Wyatt. That's not good for anybody in this town. We need to get him back or there will be consequences."

"I'll see what I can do," Rafe said. He began thumbing through information on his phone. "I've got someone, like a consultant. He's called a fixer. But it'll cost you."

"Do it."

He clicked the screen and I could hear the other line ringing. "Yeah, this is Rafe from Charmed, I'm Sure. I've got a Code Orange that I could use your help with. Can you swing by, like now-ish?"

I drummed my nails on the counter, waiting.

"Awesome, dude. You rock." He tucked his phone back into his pocket. "He'll be here in five minutes. He's kind of new, but seems awesome at what he does."

I sagged with relief. "Thank you, Rafe. I'm sorry if I was short-tempered with you. I'm just really worried about my friend."

He shrugged. "It's all good, Lady Rose. We all have our triggers, am I right? If my sister wants to see my dark side, she knows all she has to do is reset my game or change my password and not tell me the new one." He whistled. "You haven't seen Armageddon until Rafe has to reset his password with another capital letter and another symbol."

"Yeah, that's the same," I said bitterly.

I pretended to browse the other potions in the shop while I waited for the consultant. It was hard to concentrate on anything other than the impending resolution. Finally, the door swung open and the consultant stepped inside.

"Craig?"

He seemed equally surprised to see me. "Good to see you, Ember," he said.

"Are you here to buy a potion?" I asked.

"Actually, my presence was requested," Craig said. "I sometimes served as a consultant on special cases in my hometown and my employers were kind enough to give references to some of the businesses here. I have an advanced degree in mixology."

Craig was the fixer? This was not great news. I didn't want him to disclose any of this to Aunt Hyacinth. On the other hand, if he managed to restore the real Granger, then maybe it wouldn't matter. Still, I'd rather my aunt not know what really happened. The council could still decide that Granger had been reckless in taking a potion in the first place. I didn't want to take the risk.

"Well, I'm your consult," I said. I returned to the counter to show him the Forget-Me-Yes potion. I gave him a brief rundown of events.

Craig picked up the bottle to inspect it. He opened the lid and sniffed the contents. "Ah, yes. I can detect the problem."

"You can? Just like that?"

"The balance is off," he said. "This one is a very delicate, complex mixture. A fraction of an ounce in the wrong direction and you get... Well, you get your problem with the sheriff."

"Can you fix it?" I asked, my heart hammering. "Can you mix another potion that reverses the effects?"

"Absolutely," he said.

My relief was so strong that I nearly collapsed in a heap. "How long will it take?"

"If I have all the ingredients I need here, then maybe half an hour?"

I threw my arms around him. No matter what concerns I

had regarding his intentions toward my aunt, right now he was my saving grace and I was grateful.

Rafe showed us to a back room where Craig set to work at one of the potion stations. He reminded me of a bartender, the way he poured and tossed and stirred his liquids. It was plain to see that this was second nature to him.

"Does my aunt know about this?"

He glanced at me. "About the sheriff's situation?"

"No, about your side hustle. Your special skills."

"I don't think it's actually come up in conversation. I'm only called in for emergencies." He seemed to take the measure of me. "I suppose we each have a secret we might like to keep."

"Why don't you want her to know? What's wrong with being an advanced mixologist? My aunt thinks highly of anyone who excels in magic. You must've noticed that."

"Yes, but she also prizes those who don't need to earn a living, which I do." His expression softened. "She believes me to be wealthier than I am. I never lied to her, mind you, but I might have let her believe that most of my money was inherited."

Ah. That probably explained the mind reading block. He didn't want my aunt to dip into his thoughts and learn the truth. I wouldn't put it past her to try. On the other hand, she genuinely seemed to like him and it wasn't fair to build trust on a lie.

"I think you might be underestimating her, Craig. She could have easily let me move to Starry Hollow and become some sort of weird coven socialite, but she didn't. She set me up in the cottage, sure, but she also got me a job. A real job. She's disappointed in Florian when he's idle. She values hard work. She wanted to see my runecraft presentation because she wanted to see that I was working hard and earning my place." Ugh. I was defending my aunt for being my own personal taskmaster. Whatever next?

"In other words, you think I should tell her the truth," Craig said.

"Always," I said. "Ditch the mind reading block. It just makes you seem shady, like you have something sinister to hide."

He looked at me askance. "You know?"

"I may have tried to read yours," I admitted.

He grinned. "And your aunt thinks she has you pegged."

"Trust me. You don't want to start off a relationship based on lies. If you're serious about her, that's a shaky foundation to build a future on."

"A house of sand," he murmured.

"Look, Craig. The bottom line is that my aunt really seems to be into you and I don't think it's because she believes you're independently wealthy. She finds you handsome and charming and witty. That's all the real you."

"You read her mind, too, did you?" He seemed pleased to know what she thought of him.

"Tell her now before she finds out some other way. I promise you, I don't think she'll be very forgiving, no matter how much she wants to run her hands over your biceps." Inwardly, I shuddered. Now I needed a forget potion for that memory.

"Thank you for your keen insight, Ember." He handed me the completed potion. "Tell the sheriff to drink this. All of it. He should be back to his version of normal within twenty-four hours."

I accepted the bottle. "Thank you, Craig. You have no idea how much I appreciate this."

He winked. "It'll be our little secret."

"For now," I reminded him.

"For now," he agreed.

It didn't take much effort to convince Granger to drink the potion. Once I left, however, I put a spell on his doors and windows that prevented him from leaving for twenty-four hours. It was best for everyone if he stayed put and I only felt a smidge guilty about it.

After my good deed was done, I headed to the office to type up my notes on Shayna's case and call Deputy Bolan with an update.

"Coming to work at this late hour?" a voice asked. "If nothing changes, nothing changes."

"Bentley!" I'd forgotten the elf was due back from his honeymoon. "How was it?"

"Best week of my life," he said. "I can't thank Alec enough."

"You'll do your best. You wouldn't be Bentley if you didn't have your lips permanently fixed to his behind."

"My lips were there long before yours," he shot back, then seemed to realize it wasn't the zinger he thought it was. "Forget it."

I laughed. "I'm sure the honeymoon cocktails have fried a few brain cells, not that you could afford to lose any."

"It's the wedding that nearly made me lose my mind. Remind me to never plan one again."

"You barely planned this one," I said, as I typed a text to Deputy Bolan with the good news about the sheriff.

Bentley ignored me. "I understand the point of a honeymoon now. It's because a vacation is a necessity after the stress of a wedding."

"Or you could be me and get knocked up and not really have a wedding." I dropped into my chair and fired up the computer.

Bentley grimaced. "No, the wedding was important to us. Truth be told, Meadow did the hard part."

I smirked. "You don't say." I laughed at the deputy's reply to my text—a smiling leprechaun emoji.

"Meadow slept half the honeymoon. She'd been so stressed before we left. She had to keep apart squabbling relatives and ex-partners from each other, as well as from their friends." He shook his head. "I'm sorry Shayna's dead, of course, but she was one of the most difficult guests to seat. If Franco weren't Meadow's uncle, we would have just left her off the list. Every time we thought we'd handled the situation, someone else popped up."

"Tyra Langley," I said.

Bentley groaned. "Don't say that name. Meadow was disappointed that Tyra and her date left early. We paid for their meals."

"None of Shayna's ex-partners were there, though," I said.

"No, but even ex-partners of her friends were an issue," Bentley said. "I'd accidentally put Quincy Brickstone at their table and Meadow nearly had a meltdown because she knew it would cause trouble."

"Brickstone," I repeated. "As in Sonja Brickstone?"

He shot me a quizzical look. "Her ex-husband."

"This guy was at the wedding?" I asked. "He actually showed up?"

"Yes. Didn't you meet him? Medium height and build. He wore a seersucker suit with a hat. Very dapper dude. He and Meadow know each other from…"

I jumped up from my chair. "I need to go."

The elf blinked. "Go where?"

"I have another lead," I said.

"Then call Sheriff Nash."

"I can't yet," I said. "It hasn't been twenty-four hours." And I couldn't risk letting him botch the investigation.

"Twenty-four hours for what?" Bentley asked. "Does he have the flu?"

"Something like that," I yelled. Once outside, I sent another text to Deputy Bolan and rushed to my car.

CHAPTER EIGHTEEN

THE CROQUET COURT was easy enough to find. Apparently, there was only one official one in town and it was perched on a cliff overlooking Starlight Cove.

I spotted a solitary figure in a seersucker suit—this one in a pale apricot color. His hat was askew and he seemed intent on lining up the mallet in his hands. I landed my broomstick and sauntered over to greet him.

"Quincy Brickstone?"

He straightened, noticing me for the first time. He wore thick-rimmed black glasses and his shirt was partially unbuttoned at the top, as though croquet were somehow a strenuous game.

"Do I know you? You look familiar?" A sly grin spread across his face and he leaned on the mallet as though it were a cane. "You're the mosquito witch from Meadow's wedding. Fabulous performance. Five stars."

I curtsied. "That's me."

"Am I part of your apology tour?" he asked. "Poor Meadow was aghast, not that I blame her."

"Unfortunately, I'm here to talk to you about a more important matter. Shayna Masters."

His grin dissolved. "What about her?"

"You were at the wedding," I said. "You know what happened."

"I know she died," he said. "I heard she was drunk and choked on her own vomit." He shook his head. "Dreadful way to go."

"She didn't choke on vomit," I said. "She choked on a brooch. A pretty pin in a flower design. Sound familiar?"

The muscle in his cheek pulsed. "How should I know?"

"Because this one belonged to your mother."

His whole body tensed. "The brooch was…recovered?"

"From her throat, yes."

"I guess that's a silver lining in the entire bleak affair. Is there a form I need to complete to request its return?"

My mouth dropped open. His callous reaction was… telling. "The brooch doesn't belong to you, Mr. Brickstone. It belongs to Shayna Master's estate, or Sonja Brickstone, should she choose to reclaim it."

Quincy scowled at the mention of his ex-wife. "She has no right to that brooch. She should have returned it to me as part of the divorce settlement."

"You'll have to take that up with a lawyer," I said.

His brow furrowed. "So why are you here?"

I cast a glance over my shoulder, wondering where Deputy Bolan was. I hadn't received a reply to my last text, but there was no reason to assume he hadn't received it.

"Let me see if I can piece together what happened," I said, stalling for time. "You saw Shayna wearing the brooch at the wedding and it peeved you."

"That's an understatement. That brooch belonged to my mother, the legendary Patricia Brickstone." He paused dramatically, waiting for me to acknowledge the importance of that statement.

"Yes, I know. I already said that."

His face turned crimson. "That brooch is rightfully mine."

"And you decided to take it back by whatever means necessary. I get it. Misdirected anger toward your ex-wife over the divorce. Nothing new there."

"I rarely give that Amazon a second thought," he scoffed.

"So this was about money?" I asked.

Quincy leaned his hip against the handle of the mallet and removed his thick-rimmed glasses. He wiped the lenses with a crisp handkerchief. "Certainly not, how uncouth. Brickstones aren't concerned with money. That's so bourgeois."

"Then what was the issue?" I pressed.

"I don't think you're hearing me," Quincy ground out. "That brooch belonged to my *mother*. It has sentimental value. I adored her. I still remember when she got that brooch. We were in France on a culinary trip, just the two of us."

Now I understood. Quincy Brickstone was the ultimate mama's boy. "I understand that it has sentimental value, Quincy, but it's still just an object. You don't murder someone over it."

"I didn't murder anyone."

"Oh? Then what happened?"

Hatred twisted his otherwise benign features. "I spotted that brooch across the beach. That's how well I know it. I followed Shayna to the stalls so that we could have a civilized conversation. I assumed that once I explained the situation, she would simply acquiesce. What kind of cold-hearted monster wouldn't?"

"It's really Sonja you should be angry with," I said. "She kept the brooch and then, instead of returning it to you when she didn't want it anymore, she gave it to Shayna to sell. Why murder Shayna over it? She was an innocent third party."

Quincy put on his glasses. "I told you I didn't kill her."

"I beg to differ. You shoved that brooch down her throat and then strangled her until she choked on it."

He shook his head. "Why would I do that? I wanted that brooch back. I wasn't about to watch it disappear down that troll's gullet." He cringed. "Mother would be mortified if she knew what had become of it. Patricia Brickstone had more class and style in her pinky finger than that troll had in her entire enormous body."

"If you didn't kill her, then what happened?"

"That vicious woman," he said, his anger rising again. "She laughed when I told her how special that brooch was to me and that it was rightfully mine. She said that Sonja had told her I had an unhealthy obsession with my mother and that I would flip my lid if I knew she planned to sell it."

"And what did you do in response?" Because it seemed to me that Sonja was right.

"I offered to buy it, to name her price. I would have paid ten times its value. She knew I could afford it, too."

Oh no. Shayna, you didn't. "She refused?"

"She said she'd sell it to anyone except me, that I'd been horrible to Sonja during the divorce and I didn't deserve any cherished memories."

"What did you do?" I asked quietly.

"I reached for the brooch to take it from her, but she was too quick. She got to it first and popped it into her mouth."

Wow, Shayna had some spiteful bones in her body. "You're telling me that Shayna killed herself accidentally?"

"In a nutshell." He brought the mallet to rest on his shoulder.

"That doesn't explain the strangulation marks on her neck, Mr. Brickstone."

"Because I tried to get her to spit it out. I grabbed her by the neck and tried to force her mouth open. At some point during the altercation, she actually swallowed the brooch and began to choke."

"And you didn't call for help? You left her there to die?"

"I panicked. I didn't know what to do. I had no intention of killing her, no matter how monstrous she was. I only wanted the brooch back." His voice trembled. "Mother bought me my first pinstripe suit when she was wearing that brooch."

Something still didn't add up. "Quincy, when I found Shayna, she was in a portable toilet with the door closed, yet you say your altercation took place outside the stalls."

"I don't know," he replied. "I left. Maybe she went in there to throw up when she was choking."

My stomach churned. "No, Quincy. You didn't. You waited."

"I don't know what you mean."

"You waited to make sure she actually died, didn't you?" Somehow that seemed even worse than a crime of passion. Standing there dispassionately while the life drained out of her. "Quincy, you may not have been the one to choke the life out of her, but you are far from innocent."

He lowered the mallet and gripped the handle with both hands. "You can't prove that," he said. "Besides, who are they going to believe? The son of Patricia Brickstone or some half-baked witch with roots in desperate need of a touchup?"

"You're not the only one with connections to a famous family," I said. "I'm the niece of Hyacinth Rose-Muldoon. I'm a descendent of the One True Witch. Who do you think they're going to believe? The son of a socialite or the descendent of the most famous witch in history?"

"My word versus a dead witch?" he said, causing a chill to travel down my spine. "That one's easy."

He swung the mallet at my head and I ducked. My gardening skills were crap, but my reflexes were enviable. As my fingers curled around my wand, he attacked again and knocked it out of my hand. It bounced across the ground and landed next to a wicket.

Before I could reach for it, he tossed the mallet aside and lunged. His hands grasped my neck and I was surprised how strong he was for his size. I twisted and tried to reach for my wand, but his grip was too tight. I could hardly breathe, let alone move or think. I felt myself starting to lose consciousness and I knew I couldn't let that happen. If I couldn't fight back, I was as good as dead. With his fingers pressed against my windpipe, there was no chance of an incantation or even a scream. Where in the hell was Deputy Bolan? I told him croquet. How hard could it be?

You had one job, leprechaun, I thought bitterly. *The croquet court. And now I'm going to die at the hands of a man who dresses like Orville Redenbacher.*

"I'm going to get that brooch back if it's the last thing I do," he said, spitting as he spoke. He reminded me of rabid animal. Crap on a cracker, Quincy was certifiable. Killing me wouldn't get his brooch back, but logic had clearly scattered in the breeze.

I managed to raise an arm high enough to stick my thumb in his eye. I pressed as hard as I could and heard him grunt in response. He began to throttle me and I knew I didn't have much time. Anger pulsed through my body. Why did this chucklehead think his love for his mother should trump Marley's love for me? If he killed me, Marley would have no one. She'd already lost so much in her short life. I couldn't let her suffer because I wasn't strong enough to defend myself. What was the point of all this practice, of learning all this magic, when I couldn't use it to my advantage when it really mattered? I thought of Ivy and her power. Here was a witch so strong that she struck fear into the hearts of the coven. That they stripped her of it. Her blood now coursed through my veins. I was capable of much more than what I could demonstrate in a classroom. I'd never been a model student like Marley, but that didn't mean I lacked the ability. The whole reason I was in Starry Hollow now was because I was able to use magic without any training. Everyone knew I had raw, untapped power. It had certainly been discussed often enough. When I managed to escape from Jimmy the Lighter in that New Jersey driveway, I'd triggered a storm—

That was it.

I reached into my very depths and called to the energy inside me, demanded its presence. Magic stirred and I felt the power rise to greet me.

"Why won't you die?" he muttered. He was actually frustrated that he couldn't kill me as quickly as he wanted. This guy reached a whole new level of entitlement.

Thunder clapped overhead and sheets of rain came pouring down. His grip loosened thanks to the water droplets and I was able to pull away. I rushed toward the wand, but he kicked it aside so that it balanced dangerously close to the edge of the cliff. If I ran to it, I had no doubt he'd try to push me over.

Instead, we went for the mallet at the same time. He got there a split second before I did, so I rolled to the side before he could whack me with it.

"Give up, Quincy," I said, my voice hoarse. "You can't win."

He laughed. "Of course I can. I have a mallet and you're nothing without your wand." He glanced toward the cliff. "And I don't think you have the guts to get it."

She's more than just a wand, Orville Reden-whatever, a voice said.

My familiar scrambled into the clearing and launched

himself at Quincy's chest. The mallet flew to the ground and I ran to recover my wand before it plunged into the water below.

He's trying to shift, Raoul warned. The raccoon was wrapped around Quincy's chest, clawing at his eyes.

I aimed my wand at Quincy and said, *"Congelo!"*

He stood perfectly still and Raoul slid down, making sure to rip the fabric of his expensive suit on his way to the ground. The rain stopped and the clouds cleared as though nothing had happened.

Wonder twin powers, activate! Raoul said, coming over to fist bump me.

We are not twins, wondrous or otherwise.

Now is probably not the best time to take issue with my catchphrase.

"Since when is that your catchphrase?"

Quincy was frozen, his eyes stuck on me and staring as though I had two heads—which I kind of did, only one was super hairy and wearing a bandit mask.

"How did you find me?" I asked.

I was coming back through the woods after a trip to the dump, he said. *I wanted to source a matching piece for the scratching post.*

"Oh, no," I said. "Please don't."

Anyway, I felt this sense of panic and then I heard your scary voice in my head. The one you use when you're pumped full of anxiety.

The sound of a car alerted us to Deputy Bolan's arrival. The leprechaun's little legs swished back and forth as he hurried to the scene.

"What took you so long?" I demanded. "Were you deliberately waiting for him to kill me so you could arrest him after?"

Deputy Bolan shot me an aggrieved look. "Your text said

crochet, Rose. I was running all over town trying to find a place where paranormals meet to crochet."

"Stupid autocorrect," I mumbled.

"I tried calling you, but you didn't answer."

"Kind of busy not being murdered," I said, inclining my head toward a frozen Quincy. "Someone had a severe case of grabby hands." I rubbed Raoul's head. "And someone else is getting a large pizza tonight, all to himself."

Raoul tapped his paws together. *Have I mentioned we make a great team?*

Deputy Bolan walked past us to arrest Quincy. "This part's easy when they can't move. Thanks, Rose. I appreciate your help with this."

"It was the least I could do."

The leprechaun met my gaze. "That's not true and you know it. You don't owe him anything. I know I give you a hard time, but…" He trailed off. "The truth is you're not that bad."

"Ooh, high praise," I said. "Stop now, Deputy, or you might embarrass me."

Deputy Bolan tried to lead Quincy to the car, but the killer was still frozen to the ground. "Uh, a little help?"

Can I carry him? Raoul asked. *I promise to only drop him two or three times on the way.*

I used my wand to release Quincy from the spell. The moment he could move, he began to shout obscenities at me.

"Can you maybe do the spell again, but only on his mouth?" Deputy Bolan asked.

"He does have the right to remain silent." I took aim and said, "*Conquiesco.*"

Quincy's body slumped to the ground.

"Oops," I said. "Well, at least he'll be quiet."

I helped the deputy drag the limp body into the back of the police car.

"Can I give you a lift back?" the leprechaun offered.

"No, thanks. I've got my broomstick." I looked at Raoul. "How about it, trash panda? Want a ride to the cottage?"

His dark eyes blinked in disbelief. *Really? You said if I touched your broomstick again that you'd fly me over the ocean and dump my body for the sharks.*

"That was said in the heat of the moment," I said. "I promise I won't use you as shark bait."

My day is suddenly looking up. He ran to the broomstick on all fours.

I watched with satisfaction as the deputy drove away with an unconscious Quincy Brickstone. "Same, Wonder Twin. Same."

CHAPTER NINETEEN

PP3 BARKED and ran to the door.

"What now? You were just outside half an hour ago." If he was going to start having incontinence issues, I was getting him doggie diapers.

The terrier sniffed a folded note on the floor. I picked it up and opened it, immediately recognizing the handwriting.

Dear Ms. Rose,

Thank you for your assistance with the matter of great importance that we discussed at our confidential Council of Elders meeting. By all accounts, the murder has been solved and the sheriff seems to have rectified his undesirable behavior. You will be pleased to know that the council has agreed to set aside its vote of no confidence and allow Sheriff Nash to continue in his post without reservation.

Anonymously yours,
 Arthur Rutledge

. . .

P.S. - You didn't receive this from me.

P.P.S. - This note will self-destruct in one minute. Oliver helped me with the destruction spell this time, but please don't mention his name either.

The note dissolved just as I finished reading the last word. "Cut that one a bit close, Oliver," I said.

I returned to the sofa where I had been reviewing some of the chapters I'd found on Ivy in library books from Delphine.

Marley bounced into the room and plopped beside me. "Find anything helpful yet?" She seemed to ask me that every five minutes.

"Everything is so vague," I said. "No one comes right out and says what happened." If there was a passive aggressive style of writing, this was it.

"Have you found anything about her excessive force?" Marley asked.

"No specifics. Only that it was the charge against her."

"What about her personal life? Did she have a family? What was her relationship like with her parents?"

I laughed. "Slow down there, Mistress of Inquisitions. There's been no mention of anyone special."

"That's surprising," Marley said.

I cocked an eyebrow. "Is it? Why do you think so?"

"You've seen her portrait," Marley said. "She's so pretty and powerful and from a prominent family. If she wasn't involved with anyone, there had to be a reason."

She had a point. Women like Ivy Rose never lacked for suitors. So far the only insight these books provided was how advanced her magic was. She really seemed to operate at an advanced level, at least from my limited perspective.

"If you think the summoning spell helped you find the Book of Shadows, then what do you think the bees meant?"

I drummed my fingers on the open page of the book. "I'm not sure. Initially, I didn't think it had any connection to Ivy. I assumed I messed up the spell."

"But now?" Marley prompted.

"I think it was a story," I said. "About Ivy. I checked this nature book out of the library." I gestured to the book on the coffee table.

Marley's eyes widened. "You're reading about nature? Voluntarily?"

"It's about hives and queen bees," I said. "It's actually fascinating."

Marley pulled the book onto her lap and flipped to the marked pages. Her face contorted as she read. "Bees are brutal."

"Which part did you read?"

"There are bees called drones that rely on the worker bees to feed them, and at some point, they stop getting fed and starve to death."

"That's a whole different kind of teamwork."

"The worker bees also decide when it's time to create a new queen bee," Marley said. "They'll rip the stinger from the current queen so she dies."

I winced. "That's hardcore." At least the Council of Elders didn't operate like a hive or Granger would have had far worse problems than a vote of no confidence.

"I think you're right, Mom."

I balked. "I am? About what?"

"I think the summoning spell delivered a message. I think Ivy was trying to explain what happened to her." Marley's enthusiasm was infectious. She picked up another book from the library. "It tells us that she was stripped of her magic and forced to step down as High Priestess, the same way the queen was treated by the hive."

I started to process the information. "You think the coven is the hive in this scenario?"

Marley nodded, barely able to contain her excitement. "Some cultures believe that bees have magical powers."

"Like the coven," I said, more to myself. Marley definitely seemed to be on to something. "That still doesn't explain why, though. What was the excessive force? Did she deserve her punishment?"

Marley scanned the page in front of her. "I think we'll need more than symbols to figure that out."

A low growl erupted from PP3, although he remained in his place on the sofa, nestled beside me.

"Someone's here," I said. I extricated myself from the books and my family to answer the door. I was only mildly surprised to see Sheriff Nash on my doorstep. He had dark circles under his eyes and he couldn't quite bring himself to look me in the eye.

"Can we talk a minute?" he asked in a low voice. He didn't seem to want Marley to know he was here.

I stepped outside and closed the door behind me. "How are you feeling?"

"Like an ass," he said. "Thank you for everything you did. You don't know much I appreciate it."

"I'm pretty sure I do," I said. "Please don't give it another thought. I know you would've done the same for me."

He stuffed his hands into the pockets of his jeans. "I can't believe how badly I behaved. I can hardly stand the look of myself in the mirror."

"Don't beat yourself up, Granger. It was a mistake. We all make them." Some of us more than others.

"Mama sends her thanks, too." He bent down and

produced a glass jug filled with bright yellow liquid. "She told me to bring you this."

I smiled and accepted it. "Homemade lemon fizz. Tell her she's the best."

"I'm sorry I put you in that position, Rose. I'm supposed to serve and protect the community, not make you serve and protect me."

"You were only trying to take care of yourself. I totally understand that. Please don't apologize for trying to move on with your life. It was the right thing to do."

"But a foolish way to do it. I should know better than to use magic to try to fix my problems," he said. "I'm a werewolf. That's not our way."

"How's my little buddy?" I asked.

A smile tugged the corners of his lips. "He'll recover. He gave me a good kick in the pants, but I deserved it."

"So where did his foot land—at your kneecap?" I couldn't see the leprechaun getting his own leg any higher than that.

The sheriff chuckled. "About there."

A thought occurred to me. "Have you…Do you know all the women you were…?" I didn't know how to finish the question.

He sucked in an uncomfortable breath. "I don't have complete memory loss. Some parts are hazier than others and I found a few unfamiliar numbers in my phone, but I've been working my way through them. Don't want to cause anyone else heartache. I know how that feels."

"Who knows? Maybe you'll get a real date out of all this."

He pulled a face. "Any woman who wanted to date that Granger isn't really someone I'd be compatible with. I think Wyatt's going to end up reaping the benefits."

I groaned. "Of course he is."

He closed his eyes. "Rose, did I…grab your butt?"

I hesitated, debating whether to be honest. "No," I finally

said. "That must've been another woman. You were nothing but respectful to me."

He dragged a hand through his hair and exhaled. "Thank the gods. I was really hoping it wasn't you, but I couldn't remember for sure."

"Would you like to come in for a drink of lemon fizz? Marley and I are doing a little research. Nothing that can't wait."

He seemed to consider the offer. "I should probably get going. I've got a life to be getting on with, and so do you."

"You're always welcome here, Granger."

He took a reluctant step backward. "See you around, Rose." He turned and swaggered back to his car.

"I believe the name you're looking for is honeypot," I called after him.

He gave a final wave before ducking into his car and driving away.

* * *

You can preorder Magic & Misdeeds, Book 11, now!

ALSO BY ANNABEL CHASE

Thank you for reading *Magic & Maladies*! Sign up for my newsletter and receive a FREE Starry Hollow Witches short story— http://eepurl.com/ctYNzf. You can also like me on Facebook so you can find out about the next book before it's even available.

Other books by Annabel Chase include:

Spellbound Paranormal Cozy Mysteries

Curse the Day, Book 1

Doom and Broom, Book 2

Spell's Bells, Book 3

Lucky Charm, Book 4

Better Than Hex, Book 5

Cast Away, Book 6

A Touch of Magic, Book 7

A Drop in the Potion, Book 8

Hemlocked and Loaded, Book 9

All Spell Breaks Loose, Book 10

Spellbound Ever After

Crazy For Brew, Book 1

Lost That Coven Feeling, Book 2

Wands Upon A Time, Book 3

Charmed Offensive, Book 4

Poetry in Potion, Book 5

Federal Bureau of Magic cozy mystery:

Great Balls of Fury, Book 1
Fury Godmother, Book 2
No Guts, No Fury, Book 3
Grace Under Fury, Book 4
Bedtime Fury, Book 5
Three Alarm Fury, Book 6

Spellslingers Academy of Magic
Outcast, Warden of the West, Book 1
Outclassed, Warden of the West, Book 2
Outlast, Warden of the West, Book 3

Made in the USA
Monee, IL
21 June 2021